Mary Healy

Storm-driven

Vol. 2

Mary Healy

Storm-driven
Vol. 2

ISBN/EAN: 9783743357099

Manufactured in Europe, USA, Canada, Australia, Japa

Cover: Foto ©Andreas Hilbeck / pixelio.de

Manufactured and distributed by brebook publishing software (www.brebook.com)

Mary Healy

Storm-driven

BY

MARY HEALY,

AUTHOR OF "LAKEVILLE," "A SUMMER'S ROMANCE," OUT
OF THE WORLD," ETC.

IN THREE VOLUMES.

VOL. II.

London :

SAMPSON LOW, MARSTON, SEARLE, & RIVINGTON,

CROWN BUILDINGS, 188, FLEET STREET.

1876.

LONDON :
GILBERT AND RIVINGTON, PRINTERS,
ST. JOHN'S SQUARE.

CONTENTS TO VOLUME II.

CHAPTER VII.

CHAPTER VIII.

CHAPTER IX.

CHAPTER X.

CHAPTER XI.

CHAPTER XII.

CHAPTER XIII.

CHAPTER XIV.

STORM-DRIVEN.

CHAPTER I.

ONE evening, towards the end of November, Lil sat alone in Mrs. Cox's Paris salon. She was the one bit of sober quiet colour, with her plain grey dress, in all the gilt splendour of the immense room. There was gold everywhere; in the chairs, in the massive tables, gold about the huge fireplace, with its great red fire; gold about the windows, with their crimson hangings, —red and gold, gold and red. Usually in

French houses, everything, on the contrary, is on a small scale, and harmonious in tone; but in certain fashionable hotels, vast apartments are kept for very rich foreigners who want show and much finery, without the trouble of an organized household; Mrs. Cox was one of these foreigners, beloved of hotel-keepers. As Lil sat by a shaded lamp, quietly working, she looked none the less pretty for the quakerlike simplicity of her dress; her expression, however, was subdued, and she was a little pale.

The past two months, during which she had travelled with her patroness in England, before settling down in Paris, had taught her various things useful to know, but not always pleasant to learn; she had learned them, however, by heart.

Mrs. Cox was never unkind to her—that

would not have been in the lady's nature,
but more and more, day by day, she made
Lil feel that she was an inferior; now and
again the old fancy would come back, for,
after all, Lil was extremely pretty, and
very bright as a travelling-companion,
enjoying things with a freshness and
youthfulness which amused Mrs. Cox; but
the fits of affection grew less and less
frequent. She had but said the truth,
when she told Lil that she was besieged
on every side; beset by suitors; sought
out by fashionable people, or would-be
fashionable people who wanted her name
on their visiting-lists; worried by well-
dressed beggars, by tradespeople, so that
she had but very little time to herself. As
soon as it was known that she was in Paris,
cards, notes, and visits succeeded each
other in uninterrupted succession. Lil in

her capacity of secretary had plenty to
do.

Then came balls, dinners, and theatre-
going. The season had not fairly com-
menced, but where Mrs. Cox was, parties
and fashionable doings were never wanting.
Sometimes she took Lil with her, but as a
general thing she left her at home. This
evening, for instance, she was dressing to
go to a ball, where she had no intention of
taking her. Lil was quite as well pleased
that it should be so; going out in Paris
among utter strangers, who seemed to look
upon her as a very insignificant person
indeed, was quite different to those parties
in Lakeville, where she was fêted and made
much of; she was just as pretty now as
then, prettier indeed, with more softness
and womanliness in her beauty, yet no one
seemed to notice her in this new, strange

world. Quietly her needle went in and out of her embroidery; she was in that vague, not unpleasant state of mind, when no distinct thoughts shape themselves, but when images, often incongruous and un-expected, float idly before one. Suddenly the door was flung open, and a servant called out in a distinct voice,—

"Monsieur Leigh Ward."

And Leigh Ward entered.

Lil rose, and instinctively turned her face from the light. She had known that, sooner or later, this meeting must take place; but she had hoped to be better prepared for it, than she now found herself. The lamp had a heavy shade over it, and the rest of the room was in a half-obscurity, so that Leigh did not at once recognize her. He did not even know that she was with Mrs. Cox. But when he had approached quite near, he changed colour.

"Miss Temple!"

There was a moment's silence, during which the two looked at each other. Then, Lil being a woman, and very proud, managed to say quite composedly,—

"You wish to see Mrs. Cox; she is dressing, I will go and tell her that you are here," she turned from him, not choosing to notice the hand which, after the first moment's hesitation, he had held out, and walked across the large salon, towards Mrs. Cox's bed-room. This walking across the room was a most difficult task; she scarcely saw before her; but nothing in her movements betrayed this, she went as quietly as though she had been entirely mistress of herself; he noticed this, and it did not please him.

Presently she came back,—

"Mrs. Cox begs that you will wait for her; she bids me entertain you, so that the time may not seem too long."

Lil said this with a slight smile, in which was no little sarcasm; the position was a singular one, but now she was equal to it, she was entirely mistress of herself; he saw this, in the way she took up her work and threaded her needle.

"How could I find the time long near you, Miss Temple?"

He had scarcely uttered these words, when he felt how absurd and out of place such a trivial compliment was. He was angry with himself and with her, because when she raised her clear eyes to his, there was in them a sort of amused contempt, which she did not even attempt to conceal. He did not choose to risk another such a glance; he got up and went towards the fire, where moodily he warmed his feet.

After all, why should the position be so very awkward? why should she receive him with such a singular mixture of embarrassment and contempt? There had never been any engagement between them; it is true, he had been very attentive to her at one time, she was then the prettiest, freshest girl of her circle; she had attracted him even more than pretty girls usually did. He had recognized in her, feeling and intelligence; his artist nature had been moved in her presence, she had inspired him; he did not clearly remember whether or not the idea of marrying her had entered his mind; on the whole, he thought that it had not. Oddly enough, mixed with his vaguely poetic nature, there was a vein of practical shrewdness inherited

from his Yankee forefathers, and that
shrewdness had kept him free from all the
matrimonial toils which had been spread
for him. Mrs. Cox's warning long ago
had not been simply interested; Leigh
Ward really was not a marrying man. His
refinedly sensuous nature, his worship of
his own person, of his talents, of his tastes,
of all that was beautiful and artistic about
him forbade it. His ample allowance
sufficed for one; it would not, according
to his notions of life, have sufficed for
more than one.

As he stood with his back to the fire, he
revolved the past in his thoughts. If the
truth were known, he had somewhat forgotten that past; so many things had happened since then! All he clearly saw was,
that Lil had seemed to him a poetic embodiment of youth and grace at Mrs. Cox's

ball, and that later, when he had seen her trudging along in the half-melted snow, holding an umbrella, and wrapped in a hideous waterproof, she had no longer appeared to him as that same poetic embodiment. Was it his fault, if his fastidious taste disclaimed any possible connexion between waterproofs, umbrellas, and poetry?

But all this did not prevent the present state of things from being highly disagreeable, not to say ridiculous; and ridicule was a thing which this man could not brook. Shaking back his hair from his brow, where it was apt to fall in curling disorder, he suddenly left his position before the fire, and, drawing up a chair, he sat down close to Lil and began playing with her embroidery.

"Miss Temple, why do you receive me

so unkindly? Why are you so unlike yourself?"

Lil wished he had remained by the fire. She wished his voice did not sound so sweet, so persuasive in her ears; he was nothing to her now; she did not care for him more than for the stranger passing in the street; but the modulations of that voice brought back to her all the past with its foolish dreams and its proud security so vividly, that a great longing to cry came upon her. But she must not show this; it might be misconstrued; so after a moment's hesitation, during which she made a few abominably irregular stitches, she said quietly enough, but in a low voice,—

"Because, Mr. Ward, I am not in reality my old self; because the Lil Temple you knew, was a different being from the Lil Temple who is now speaking to you."

"How so?"

"Because my surroundings are different; and you know—you more than others—that one's surroundings form a part of oneself. When you knew me, and—and sought my society, I was—or was thought to be—a rich girl; there was an atmosphere of luxury about me."

"You are unjust!" he cried.

"Pardon me; I do not think I am. I do not mean that you were aware you sought my society because I had money; that would have been coarse and vulgar, and you hate coarseness and vulgarity of motives, as much—more, perhaps—than you do coarseness in dress, or food, or lodging. All I meant to say was, that I was then of your world, and that now I am not. I am glad to have this explanation with you. Frankness is always best. I do not mean to forget the change in our positions, and I do not intend that you should forget it either."

She was trembling a little now, and he, on his side, was not quite master of himself.

"I do not see—" he began, but she quickly interrupted him.

"But you must see! I am no longer a young lady in society; I am Mrs. Cox's companion—a little more than her maid. I believe we receive the same wages. The very clothes I wear were given to me by her, out of charity. I am a dependent, a hireling. My mistress says to me, Do this, and I do it; if she were to order me to unbutton her boots, I dare say I should obey; for she has bought my time, my will, my pride. I knew this all very well when I agreed to the bargain." She said this with passionate vehemence. It was better, at any rate, he thought, than her cool composure of just now; it gave him a little sense of superiority.

"All this is an indirect way to let me know that you consider me a mercenary wretch, and that you wish me to know I behaved very badly to you, after the terrible misfortunes which befell you a year ago. But I assure you that it was only a sense of delicacy—of exaggerated delicacy, perhaps—which kept me from forcing myself on your notice. Had I not left Lakeville immediately—"

"You would have left another card or two on me—I am sure of it. As it was, you did everything necessary in such a case, did you not? I am sure no book on etiquette would have counselled more. You called immediately; I even saw you

once at the old house, did I not? More
still! you sent me a most exquisite basket
of flowers in midwinter; and we all know
that flowers at that time are very expensive. You arranged them yourself, I am
sure; for none but an artist could have
combined so beautiful a disposition of
colours; and yet you did not even put
your card among the flowers, fearing that
I might deem it necessary to thank you.
Could delicacy be carried farther? No,
certainly! you omitted nothing which you
should have done, except perhaps—yes,
perhaps you ought to have found a moment to leave a P. P. C. when you went
away. I think the book on etiquette
would have counselled a P. P. C."

"When you are calmer, Miss Temple,
you will perhaps deign to listen to me."

"Calmer, Mr. Ward?" exclaimed Lil,

with a candid surprise, which would have done credit to a more experienced actress. " If I were not perfectly calm, I could not thread this needle as I am doing."

He was bitterly mortified ; he had had the worst in this encounter, and his vanity was sorely wounded. Besides, Lil had never seemed to him so beautiful as she had seemed to him in her anger. He caught a glimpse of depths in her nature which he had never suspected. In the midst of his mortification he was puzzled, likewise, about the flowers. Flowers artistically arranged ? He had not sent them ; some one else, then, had paid her this delicate attention ; some one who was perhaps in love with her. Who was it ? He puzzled over it some time. Other young men, besides himself, had paid attentions to Lil in the days of her prosperity :

which of them had sent these flowers? Then suddenly he remembered that Mr. Bruce, the painter, at Mrs. Cox's ball, had followed the young girl with his eyes wherever she went. The flowers had been artistically arranged, she said; the thought was singularly disagreeable to him. That fellow was in Paris, he knew; people were beginning to talk about him as very clever, as a future great man. One could make a nice little story out of the loves of this poor artist and of this pretty girl—for she was pretty, more than pretty! He glanced at her once more, and, with an impatient gesture, went back to the warming of his feet. But this occupation had lost its charm; he was ill at ease; the silence weighed on him; yet, with all his tact, he did not know how to break it. Soon he opened the piano and began to play;

he had found a vent to his feelings more effective than words.

Soon Lil's work dropped on her lap. It was with his music that he had first charmed her. In the early days of their acquaintance he used to play for her often, play and talk, while she sat near him. She remembered now, as she thought of that past time, with what pleasure she had listened both to the talk and to the music. The talk was principally about himself, but this seemed natural; it had a peculiar charm, for he would very frankly acknowledge his faults, declare that he was a spoiled child of fortune; that had he been forced to work for his daily bread, he might have become somebody—an artist, instead of a dilettante, a worker instead of a dabbler in many things. The real truth was, that he was quite satisfied with his dilettantism; it made him the most popular man of his set, and that popularity had become a necessity to him. Yet, when he was by her side he would deplore his want of high purpose, and there really seemed to be a sort of sincerity in the lament. All through life he had, by fits and starts, been in earnest; only it never lasted long. Impressions were so vivid with him, his sensitive nature so easily yielded to the influence of the moment, that sometimes he even deceived himself.

In a mirror, above the piano, Leigh Ward watched the young girl. He saw the studied calm of her face melt away; he saw the work fall from her hands; he saw the eyes grow dreamy and then fill with tears. Never had he been so near to real artistic excellence as at that moment; it was not on the keys merely that he was playing, it was on the sensitive heart of the girl who had dared to brave him.

"Excellent! beautifully played, Leigh!" said the clear, cold voice of Mrs. Cox, as she rustled in; "Orpheus melting his rocks was nothing to you: what passion, what force! whose peace are you attacking— mine?"

"I was endeavouring to win you from your mirror, most beautiful lady, and I have succeeded," he kissed her hand gallantly.

"I take you with me, you know; you are in so gallant a mood that I intend to profit by it."

"But I am not invited."

"If I take you there is no need of invitation. You are in evening dress, so you have no reason to refuse. Do you know that you are almost the only American who

pays me the compliment of putting on a
dress-coat for my particular benefit? Lil,"
she said, without turning round, " do come
and see what is the matter with this clasp,"
and she held out her wrist, on which shone
a diamond bracelet.

Lil came forward, and was able to arrange
the clasp with firm fingers. Mrs. Cox gave
her a furtively sharp look; but she discovered nothing, save that she was a little
paler than usual.

" By the way, Mr. Ward is an old
acquaintance of yours, is he not?"

" Yes," answered she, without looking
up from her task.

" I did not tell you in my note, that I
had engaged Miss Temple as companion,
did I? but then I had so many things to
say, that I forgot it! Come, the carriage
is waiting. Go to bed, Lil; you are pale

to-night: do not remain up novel reading, that is a dangerous sort of occupation for you, my dear," and with a careless nod, she swept out of the room, followed by Leigh.

At the carriage, however, she discovered that she had left her fan upstairs; she was going to send a servant for it, but before she could give the order, Mr. Ward was already on the stairs. He knocked at the door of the salon, but receiving no answer, he walked in.

Lil had heard nothing; she was sobbing violently, crouching by the fire, in an attitude of utter abandonment.

"Lil!" exclaimed the young man, really moved.

She uttered a slight scream, and started to her feet; she faced him, with her beautiful, tear-filled eyes full of terror, and full of passionate indignation as well.

There was no studied calmness now, no attempt at concealment.

"It is dishonourable, it is cowardly of you to surprise me so! Your vanity had been wounded, had it not? and you wanted to soothe it; there is no hiding my misery now, is there? you are right, I was crying because of you, crying to think that in my ignorance of the world, I should have given freely, joyfully, the first love, the dream of my girlhood, to a man to whom all that was but a moment's pastime; who flirted with me when he thought me rich, who deserted me when I became poor; who now, to-day, finding me in a rank of life where rich men rarely take their wives, asks nothing better than to renew that flirtation! But I am safe from you, Mr. Ward, because I despise and I hate you."

"No, Lil, you do not hate me;" he had

scarcely heard her words, he could only look at her, admiring her beauty, enhanced as it was by her passion. "No, Lil, you do not hate me," he repeated; then suddenly, before she could guess his intention, he had seized both her hands, and covered them with kisses.

An instant later, he was gone.

CHAPTER II.

WARNED.

"Lil," said Mrs. Cox, a few days after this ; "Lil, my dear, do you know that your behaviour towards Mr. Ward is very absurd?" She was trying the effect of a new bonnet before the mirror, and as she said these words she did not even turn round to look at her companion, who was seated at the table, writing notes.

"How, absurd?" asked the young girl, with a steadiness in her voice which astonished herself.

"I will tell you." The effect of the new

bonnet being satisfactory, Mrs. Cox was in a particularly good-natured frame of mind; she sat down by the fire, and looked alternately at the blazing logs, and at Lil, whom she was now facing. "You should, of course, be reserved with him, indeed I should require that of you. But that you should pointedly avoid him, that you should appear not to see when he offers to shake hands with you, that, on the slightest pretext, you should leave the room, and stay away until I am forced to send for you, —all that is absurd."

"Mr. Ward comes here as your visitor, not as mine," interrupted Lil.

"Naturally he does; but your duty, as my companion, is to remain with me when I receive visits, unless I expressly signify to you the contrary wish. Come, Lil, this is mere skirmishing; your avoidance of Mr. Ward is the avoidance of a girl who is mortally offended at what she considers a lover's desertion."

" Mrs. Cox !" exclaimed Lil, while a hot, angry flush spread over her face.

" Yes, my dear ; restrain yourself, for I have not said my say, and I mean to do so. Leigh made love to you, once."

"I beg your pardon, Mrs. Cox," said Lil, who had recovered her composure; "Mr. Ward never spoke of love to me; flirtations are too common among us Americans, to be called love-making."

" That is true. But the flirtation was becoming a very serious one. I warned you, I remember, that he was not a marrying man, and my warning was a just one; but he was certainly, the evening of my ball, in love with you—it might have drifted into matrimony for your misfortune and his— had not—"

" Had not I become a poor little nobody,

whom Mr. Leigh Ward felt to be beneath his notice."

"Now, how unjust that is!" said Mrs. Cox, looking contemplatively into the fire, and seemingly taking it into her confidence. "You are like all people who have been unfortunate, and who, on that account, accuse the rest of the world of selfishness, of heartlessness, of all sorts of ugly and disagreeable faults; whereas, it is circumstances which alone are responsible for any change which may have taken place. If you think that Lil Temple, my companion, is the same person whom Leigh Ward knew and liked ages ago, you are vastly mistaken; to him, to me, to the world in general, your personality changed with your fortunes. You think he was heartless, because he did not pursue you with his love-making to the barn where you and

your sister taught school. But Leigh
Ward is a man of fastidious tastes, of an
artistic temperament ; you, a rich girl,
answered to certain wants of that nature,
and pleased those fastidious tastes. Circumstances changed ; he changed also : it
is not he whom you should blame, it is
those circumstances."

" It is very unreasonable of us, the unfortunate ones, not to understand all this—it
is so simple," said Lil bitterly.

" Certainly, it is unreasonable ! We
worldly people are not half as bad as you
would make us out ; only do not ask heroism of us. As to Leigh, he has good qua-
lities, or rather the beginning of good qua-
lities ; he has been fortune-spoiled, but the
spoiling has left him one of the most charming men to have about one that I know.
When I first knew him, he tried to make

love to me, of course; all men begin by that. But he soon understood that he was losing his time, and accepted the place assigned to him. I wish him to represent America in my set; not that he is a typical American by any means, but because he is a pleasant specimen. Should he become poor by ill-luck, it would be like the prick of a pin in one of those pretty red balloons children play with. He is a creature of luxury, of warm and rich surroundings; it is that which attracts him to my side, it is that which has kept him from yours."

"You make him out more despicable than even I could have done!" exclaimed Lil, playing nervously with the note she had written.

"Not at all. I only see him as he is; you see him in a false light still, and the glimpses you catch of his real nature throw

you into fits of indignation : and this brings
me to what I wished to say to you ; your
exaggerated avoidance of him is not calculated to insure his indifference, and I am
sure that you are too sensible a girl to wish
for anything but indifference from him.
You are still very ignorant of the world and
its ways—amazingly so, indeed—but you
must know that when a man like Leigh
makes love to a girl in your position, it is,
as we heard them say last evening at the
Français, for " l'autre motif." Remember
what I told you on board the boat : at the
slightest appearance of irregularity in your
conduct, I should be pitiless ; and now,
my dear child," she continued airily, not
noticing Lil's sudden deadly pallor, " are
these notes written ? "

" Yes ; here they are," Lil managed to
say.

"Then, here is a list of names for my dinner invitations. I have decided on next Thursday, and I mean it to be a grand affair. By the way, you will find the name of your steam-boat friend on the list; he is in Paris, it seems. This bonnet is decidedly becoming, is it not?"

"Very becoming!" answered Lil; and there was a short silence, during which Mrs. Cox continued to admire herself in the mirror. Then she said, relapsing into a meditative mood, "And to think that once I was a poor girl like you, with no better prospects in life than yours at the present moment,—yet now! Do you know that beauty is a wonderful help to a woman, when she is clever? Men are so easily turned and turned again, if one only takes the trouble to study them a little; even ugly women succeed, think then how easy it is to the pretty ones! Come, dear! you shall write the cards this evening; it will be time enough. People break other engagements willingly to come to my dinners, therefore we need be in no hurry. Put on your bonnet, and we will take a turn in the 'Bois'; the carriage must be waiting already. If we should happen to meet Leigh Ward, we will bring him home to dinner; it will be a good opportunity to see if you understand my instructions. You know, Lil, I am really fond of you, my dear!" and this good-natured lady kissed her dependent lightly on the cheek.

They did meet Leigh Ward at the "Bois," and they brought him back to dinner, where he showed himself more amusing, more sprightly than ever. Lil joined in the conversation now and then without affectation, and won an approving glance from her patroness.

"You have forgiven me, have you not? believe that my respect for you is as great as my admiration, — believe it, I beg," whispered Leigh, as she helped him to coffee after dinner. "If I seemed to forget that respect a moment, the other evening, it was that I was not quite myself, — you were so lovely in your anger."

"What is that you are saying to Lil? I will have no asides, Leigh!"

"I was asking Miss Temple, whether she had heard from her sister lately."

"Oh! by the way, Lil, how is Martha?"

"She is very well, Mrs. Cox, thank you," said Lil, with a defiant look in her eyes; "I had a letter yesterday, in which she says that she is getting so clever in the millinery business, that she hopes to set up for herself some day."

"Indeed! when I go back to Lakeville I shall certainly order my bonnets of her, should she carry out her plan."

"That would be very kind of you, it would help us greatly; I say us, for of course I should go and help her—I should be her shop-girl."

"Quite right, my dear. Mr. Ward, my coffee is not sweet enough; do hand me the sugar."

Lil's cheeks burned; she who had been so sensitive on the subject of their social fall, now seemed to seek every occasion of parading it, of forcing her old lover to re-member the distance which existed between them. After this, however, she subsided once more into silence, and sat working by the shaded lamp, while Mrs. Cox and Leigh

Ward talked lightly together. Then visitors were announced, and once more Leigh found his way to her: she looked him full in the eyes, and said in a low, determined voice,—

"Mr. Ward, I have not forgiven you! let there be no repetition of that scene; you are to remember that I am companion to Mrs. Cox, and that as such, there can be nothing in common between you and me."

He seemed about to protest, but a look of hers checked him; he turned and left her. He was not entirely dissatisfied; in that look, mingling with the determination her words had expressed, there had been a sort of wild entreaty which he perfectly understood.

CHAPTER III.

MRS. COX'S DINNER-PARTY.

LIL was not always unhappy during this time; she had at intervals, bitter fits of crying; in certain moods, all things looked dark and sad enough, yet with it all she certainly was not entirely unhappy since that evening when Leigh Ward had found her sobbing, and had so passionately kissed her hands. He had shown himself so respectful, so diffident even, that little by little her fear of him faded away. She was so young, she so naturally craved pleasure and happiness, that there were

times when she quite forgot the humilia-
tions of her position; when she was the
Lil Temple of old,—softly gay, brightly
happy. During these moods, Mrs. Cox's
warning seemed to her quite unworthy of
remembrance. Her experience of life was
so incomplete, she was so entirely honest
and straightforward herself, that she
could not well understand that others
should act a part, and hide evil intentions
under a pleasing exterior. Americans,
she had always heard, were known for
their honourable conduct towards women,
and Mr. Ward was an American; why
should he be an exception? in other moods,
again, she would become frightened, and
then her one thought was to go away, to
get back, somehow or other, to her sister's
side, where she would be safe; safe from
the fascination of constant companionship,

safe from the seduction of his whispered words, of his looks which were constantly resting on her, till she blushed and grew uneasy. But still, she made no effort to get back to her sister; it seemed to her that she was floating down a stream, and that no effort of hers could make her gain the shore.

Mrs. Cox, had ordered her to be natural in her intercourse with her old lover; at first this had been very difficult, but soon it grew easier. They met continually: Mrs. Cox nearly always took her to the theatre when she went. There she heard music which moved her greatly, she saw acting which fascinated her; and lived more and more in a world unreal but delightful,—a world in which she always found Leigh Ward by her side.

Did he know what he was doing? probably not. He found her strangely charming with her varying moods; he yielded to the fascination,—that was all. His poet nature craved its natural food, and he took it where he found it. Had he met Lil working humbly as her sister was working, in shabby clothes, and in the midst of poor, mean surroundings, he would never have noticed her; except, perhaps, by a retrospective sigh, when he remembered what she had been. But he had not met her thus; the way in which she forced him to recognize her position, in which she made him understand that the luxury in which she lived was luxury which did not belong to her,—only added a zest to the charm which he recognized in her. Was he responsible for circumstances over which he had no control?

Mrs. Cox prided herself on her dinners,

and not without reason; and, as she had predicted, her invitations for the following Thursday were universally accepted.

The dining-room attached to her apartment was large enough to contain many guests. The best-trained servants of the hotel were at her orders. The head-cook passed a sleepless night composing a "menu" which would have done honour, as he himself expressed it, to Napoleon's table, had Napoleon still been reigning at the Tuileries. The most exquisite flowers of Paris were ordered for the occasion, and the hostess's own toilette was a triumph of its kind.

"I suppose I must make up my mind soon," she said; "decidedly, my name will not do much longer; at my table to-morrow I shall assemble all the aspirants,—at least, all those who are in Paris;

you look at them attentively and give me
your opinion. Rumour says, that Lord
Dolphus is to have the preference, but I
am by no means sure that rumour is right.
When I was your age, and poor as you
are, do you fancy Lord Dolphus would
have followed me about from place to
place, as he does? I was handsomer then
than now, for certainly youth is no detri-
ment to a woman,—but, my dear, there
was no golden halo about me in those
days! Dollars, dollars! there is nothing
in life to replace them. The golden calf has
more worshippers now than it ever had."

"You, among them," said Lil, who had
heard many such tirades of late.

"I among them," said Mrs. Cox
placidly; "quite right, Lil. There is not
a woman in, or out, of the United States,
who so well understands the value of

money, who more dearly cherishes hers, or who keeps it with more tender care. Money is everything to me; it secures respectability, it means power, it renews youth; people will consider me young for years to come, unless by ill chance I should lose my fortune; it means beauty, it is a better preservative of one's complexion than Rachel's waters and paints—though they are not to be despised either."

Lil's dress for the occasion was as simple as even a companion's dress need ever be; but it was made by one of the best dressmakers of Paris; she would not have been a woman and young, had the reflection of her beauty in the mirror given her no thrill of satisfaction. But she had no ornaments whatever, not even a locket, not even a little band of gold for her wrist; Mrs. Cox had given her nothing of

the kind; it was absurd, but Lil was
troubled by this; not even the fresh, pure-
tinted camelia in her dark hair, quite
consoled her. What did console her a
little, however, was Leigh Ward's look
of genuine pleasure and admiration when
his eyes rested on her.

Yet, when the guests had all assembled,
no one, Mr. Ward least of all, paid much
attention to the young companion. The
diamonds and gorgeous dresses of the few
ladies invited—Mrs. Cox invited women
from a sense of duty; men, because she
liked to have them about her,—crushed
the white simplicity of her toilette. When
she was seated at table, she found herself
between a German baron blessed with a
fine appetite, and a young English attaché
who honoured her with a stare, through
his one eye-glass.

"Been long in Pā-ris, Miss—? I beg your pardon."

"Miss Temple. I have been in Paris as long as Mrs. Cox, since I am her companion," retorted Lil, with that morbid pride of hers which made her fear to be taken for what she was not.

"Aw—ah!—indeed!" and the English attaché, with that fear of derogating which characterizes such beings, relapsed into silence, and the contemplation of his soup-plate.

Lil glanced at him with her eyes full of the contempt she felt; and then, her glance passed from him to a face just opposite, a face puckered and wrinkled, but brightened by a look of infinite amusement. She had scarcely seen Mr. Smith till then; he had been one of a group that came in at the last minute, and her attention had been absorbed in watching Mr. Ward fluttering about the bejewelled ladies. She blushed and smiled; she felt comforted by his hearty recognition of her, yet abashed too, when she remembered her mistake about him.

This dinner,—to which Lil had rather looked forward, as young people instinctively do look forward to festivities of any kind,—proved to be a very dull and painful affair to her. She could not watch Mr. Ward, for he was on the same side of the table as herself; she could only hear the sound of his voice, or of his low musical laugh, in the pauses of the general hum; she had plenty of leisure to listen for that voice, as, save when the German baron recommended certain dishes to her, proving at the same time, his own thorough appreciation of them, she was

left pretty well to her own resources.
Mr. Smith was, on the other hand, so
occupied in following the fluent discourse
of the young lady by his side, that all he
could do was to glance rapidly at Lil,
now and again. At last, having nothing
better to do, she found herself listening
to those two, isolating the sound of their
voices, as one can easily do, in the midst
of much noise. The young lady, the only
unmarried woman of the party except
herself, was handsome enough, but she
lacked freshness, and had forgotten, many
years before, what the word timidity might
mean ; she seemed to have made up her
mind that her neighbour should hear, see,
think of nothing but herself. Lil soon
made out that she was glibly reproaching
him for having neglected her and her
mother since his arrival in Paris.

"We did not even know that you were
in Europe; perhaps we might have remained in our ignorance, had we not found
you here, at Mrs. Cox's table. I never
was so surprised in my life."

"Nor so delighted?" asked Mr. Smith
drily.

"Nor so delighted, of course! need
you ask?" and she laughed a clear laugh,
but too loud. "But tell me—why should
you come here, when you are known to
refuse all such invitations? what is the
attraction? do tell me."

"Is it not easy to discover? it is said
that no man can approach Mrs. Cox and
her diamonds without falling immediately
in love with her—and them; why should I
be an exception? I understand she refuses
offers every day, even by telegraph; and
has to keep a secretary to answer all her

aspirants in the negative. I prefer receiving my answer from herself, and so I came. Fine woman, Mrs. Cox!"

" Yes; mamma says she really was handsome—twenty years ago."

" And is handsome still. After all, Smith does not sound much worse than Cox, does it? I am not good-looking I own, but I am not so bad as old Cox was."

" She would not have you."

" You think not?"

" She wants a title; she told mamma so. Indeed, she tells her affairs to everybody—if you propose to her, it will not long be a secret."

" Then I will not propose."

" Was Mr. Cox so very dreadful?" asked the young lady curiously, evidently deliberating whether she would have done as their hostess had done.

"That depends upon what one calls dreadful. He was rich—the marriage was a bargain, and she stuck to her engagements like a trump—better than most women would have done in such a case; now she has her reward. I do not blame her for having made the bargain, do you?" he asked, in his abrupt way.

"I?" exclaimed the girl, on the point of being frank, then remembering herself, she added, turning up her eyes, "I marry except for love? oh, never!"

"That's right," said Mr. Smith, with an odd smile; "would you believe it, Miss Blair? I, with my wrinkles and my grey hairs, am the most sentimental, soft-hearted old fool in creation. If I could be sure of being loved for myself—not for my dollars; really for myself, by some pretty girl or other—as pretty as you, for instance—I should be half-mad for joy."

Miss Blair for once in her life did not know what to answer; was it a sort of declaration, or was Mr. Smith making fun of her? she tried hard to blush, as she looked down sentimentally at the flowers by her plate, but she did not succeed.

At last the dinner, which Lil had thought interminable, came to an end. To pour out the coffee, to have something to do, was an immense relief; her movements were so graceful, she was in reality so very pretty, with her dark-fringed blue eyes, and her mass of dark hair, that more than one seemed disposed to approach her.

"Lil, get me my fan—Lil do this, do that—" and Lil would obey. Mrs. Cox

did not mean Lil or others to forget her
position.

Lil understood it all, and her heart
grew hard within her. Leigh Ward did
not even look at her; he devoted himself
exclusively to Miss Blair. So, when her
duties were over, she went and sat down
outside of the laughing circle, feeling all
the bitterness of solitude in a crowd.
There was a choking sensation in her
throat, but no one would have guessed it
from her impassible face; she turned over
the pages of an illustrated book, never noticing that she was holding it upside down.

Presently she felt that Mr. Smith had
taken a chair by her; but she did not
look up : he seemed quite satisfied to sit
there in silence as he had often done on
board the steamer. Finally he said, with
his usual abruptness,—

"Miss Blair is handsome, is she not?"

"Yes," answered Lil indifferently.

"You are not enthusiastic; what have you against her?"

"I?" she said, looking up; "nothing; she is in one world, and I in another: why should I even take the trouble to judge her?"

"But you do judge her; as one woman always judges another—give me the benefit of your observations."

"Oh! certainly. She has, 'I want a husband,' written on her face; gleaming from her eyes, ringing in her laugh, displayed among her laces. . . ."

"Well, every woman ought to have a husband, I suppose."

"Perhaps."

"Does she want that handsome fellow who is talking to her? or rather being talked to by her? Who is he?"

Lil did not need to look up, she knew who the " handsome fellow " was, but she answered steadily,—

" It is he who represents the American element in Mrs. Cox's human ménagerie— I use her own expression; she chose him because he has nice hands and feet, and does not look like a pork-packer."

" Hum ! and what element does that man by Mrs. Cox represent ? "

" The one who looks like a jockey ? he represents the English element. It is Lord Dolphus."

" Ah ! I have heard of him, a man of unpleasant antecedents, but of unexceptional family."

" Exactly."

" Go on. You know I am a stranger here."

" The German element sat by me at table ;

but he has not much chance of success, because at dinner he pays his court to the dishes, rather than to the lady; after dinner, however, he is tenderness and devotion itself."

Mr. Smith looked straight at Lil, then he shook his head, and in a changed voice he said, as he had said once before,—

" Poor little girl! poor little girl ! "

Lil glanced up quickly, then immediately resumed the study of the illustrated book, which was still upside down. For some minutes both were silent; after a while he said,—

" Miss Temple, you promised to help me if I got into trouble; could you lend me ten dollars ? "

Lil blushed, then she looked him full in in the eyes; she wanted a pretext for venting all the angry feelings within her, and the pretext offered was as good a one as any; she said rapidly,—

"It was ungenerous, it was unmanly of of you, to play that comedy with me! Is it because I am poor that people feel it to be their right to amuse themselves at my expense? That these worldlings should make me feel that I am a nobody; that they, who, were I a rich girl, would flatter and follow me, delight in my youth, declare that I was pretty; that they should form a charmed circle about them, forbidding me to enter it—that is natural, but I expected better things of you. If you are a rich man and courted, you were once poor; and you ought to feel for those who are not among the fortunate ones of the world."

"My child," he said very gravely, "believe, that if I recalled a time which was very pleasant to me, it was not with

any intention of wounding you. I felt
drawn to you then, and I feel drawn to you
now. I am a rough fellow, but I want you
to understand, that I respect and esteem
you infinitely more than any of the fine
ladies here. When I look at you and then
at them, I cannot help thinking of the
words, 'Solomon in all his glory was not
arrayed like one of these.' You are just
like your name."

He stopped, astonished at his own eloquence; but presently, as Lil did not answer,
he went on,—

" Only, there is something that pains me
in you; this life is telling on your nature;
making you less gentle, giving a sharpness
to your tongue, which before it had not.
Then, why should you force people so to
recognize your dependent position? You
quite frightened the young gentleman with

a low-necked shirt, at table! Believe me, people are not as bad or as heartless as you now think them; only they do not like to have disagreeable subjects thrust at them, and misfortune and poverty are disagreeable subjects—now, are they not? Give me your hand, to show me that you have forgiven me."

She gave him her hand, but still did not speak; she felt that if she attempted to say a word, she would surely begin to cry. He saw this, and said cheerfully,—

"Do you know that I do not find my business as tourist so very unpleasant after all? I have found a new occupation."

"Indeed?"

"You would never guess what it is—I have taken to studying art." Lil fairly laughed; Mr. Barnard Smith as an art-student was irresistibly comic.

" It is not very polite to laugh at a man like that, you know, Miss Temple! Why should I not have a gallery like others? So far, I do not care much for pictures and statues, but I dare say I shall in time; I mean to study up the art question, just as I should study up the land question in a new locality where I meant to invest. People are not such fools as one often takes them to be; they would not pay out thousands of dollars for a few daubs of bright paint on a canvas, if the daubs of paint were not worth it. I do not mean to be taken in by the first adventurer I meet; I shall learn to know the difference between—a—what do they call the fellow?—a Gérome and a Meissonier. I mean to become a patron of home talent—send out students to Italy."

" You would do this?" exclaimed Lil with sudden eagerness.

" Certainly. Have you any interesting, struggling genius to recommend ? "

" That I have ! " and she told him about Issy Richards..

" And they were really good to you and your sister, when you needed help ? "

" Yes; indeed they were ! They rather scolded me, and despised me a little, I think, but they did for us what no one else dreamed of doing."

" All right. What ought she to have a-year ? This is your affair; you have but to write to her to come out at once, and whatever orders you give to my banker for her, shall be obeyed."

" You are in earnest ? " exclaimed Lil, looking up at him with such bright grati-tude, that he wished she had a dozen more artistic protégées to recommend.

" Certainly I am. Do I look like a man

who makes promises for the sake of breaking them ? But to return to the question of my personal education, will you not help me to become a connoisseur ? "

" I am as ignorant as you. The pictures I like to look at, it seems, are those on which I ought to turn my back."

" Very well, let us pursue our studies together. But we should have some one to put us on the right track, I suppose."

" I know a very clever artist, and he is in Paris; but I do not know where, he no longer comes to see Mrs. Cox."

" Why not ? "

" Once, he called on her wearing a split glove. Mrs. Cox does not like men who wear split gloves."

" Indeed ? " and deliberately he took out a penknife and slit open his own glove.

"Do you think Mrs. Cox will shut her door on me too?"

"I think not."

"We shall see," and gravely Mr. Smith rose and went towards the mistress of the house; "Mrs. Cox," he said, "I want you to lend me Miss Temple to-morrow, that we may go to the Louvre to study art."

"Impossible! my dear Mr. Smith, quite impossible!"

"Why so?" asked Mr. Smith, undisturbed, and playing with his outrageously cut glove.

"Lil is indispensable to me, dear child! and then in Paris, young girls may not go out alone with gentlemen; it would not be proper."

But Mr. Barnard Smith was not a man who easily took a denial. Mrs. Cox of

course yielded, as she had meant all the
time to do ; so it was arranged that the
next day Mr. Smith should call for Miss
Temple.

CHAPTER IV.

ART-STUDENTS.

Mrs. Cox was perfectly sincere in her
desire for what she considered Lil's good.
A rich husband! what could a girl wish
for more than that? and Mr. Smith was
evidently much taken with the young girl.
A little skilful manœuvring, and the thing
was sure to be done. Mrs. Cox, like all
good-natured people, much preferred seeing those about her prosperous and blessed
with this world's goods, than poor and
anxious; if she could, without interfering
with her own comfort, promote that de-

sirable state of things, it was with great satisfaction she did so. She did not wish Lil to marry Leigh Ward, because he belonged to her; he was useful to her, she liked to have him at her beck and call, and she did not allow any hunting on her grounds. But Mr. Smith did not belong to her; in the first place, he was not fascinated by her, as most men were; neither her diamonds nor her smiles dazzled him. This was a matter of astonishment to her, when she thought of it; but it did not make her angry, she could afford to be generous. Besides, he was not calculated to adorn her choice circle, except in as much as his immense wealth gave him importance. His appearance was against him, even in dress-coat and white cravat he managed to look odd; by the side of the young men of the day, who displayed as much of their throats as circumstances would permit, his high, stiff, old-fashioned shirt-collar seemed ridiculous. Then his rough iron-grey beard was cut in that deplorable American fashion, which consists in leaving the upper lip and most of the chin quite bare, while the whiskers and beard join in hideous partnership. That Lil might object to these peculiarities did not enter her mind. As a husband, Mr. Smith would do very well. Did she not herself marry a man much older than herself, and far more seriously disagreeable than Barnard Smith?

All this, of course, Mrs. Cox kept to herself. Lil, she knew, had some absurd ideas about love and marriage, and she had to be managed, so she avoided talking much about her Mr. Smith; only her tirades against poverty, and her praise of wealth, and the power which wealth bestows, became still more frequent. Lil, on her side, was grateful to Mr. Smith for his notice of her, at a time when she was certainly not spoiled by too much notice. So when he came for her she was quite ready, and bright with the anticipation of a little liberty, a respite from her life of bondage.

"Take my arm, Miss Lily:" she obeyed. "Do you feel up to the study of art this morning?"

"Oh, quite; I have just been reading all that Murray says about the Louvre."

"So have I." They looked at each other and laughed.

Mrs. Cox was not a haunter of galleries; she cared as little about pictures and statues, as she did about books. So it happened that this was the first time Lil had visited the Louvre. In spite of the Murray studies, our tourists soon lost their way in the different rooms.

"We must steer for the " Salon Carré," said Mr. Smith, studying his guide-book and pronouncing in a way which made Lil smile.

They were at that moment looking at the pictures of the French school, quite unconscious that the Pierrot of Watteau was not an " old master." But Lil, whose French was really good, accosted a dignified official, and they at last found themselves where Murray told them they should go.

Lil had not exaggerated when she confessed that she knew nothing about pictures. Those who imagine that appreciation of art is a natural instinct, quite apart from education, make a great mistake. Dimly, as she stood in that wonderful room, she felt that there was a world of which she knew nothing opening before her, which attracted her with a half-pleasing, half-frightening fascination. But with the instinctive preference for what is pretty rather than for what is severe, she turned from Leonardo da Vinci, from Holbein and Raphael, to stand in admiration before the Murillo. Perhaps, the number of copyists crowded about the picture helped her in her choice.

"How lovely, is it not?" she exclaimed.

"Hum! let's see what Murray says of it," answered Mr. Smith, who would not compromise himself, and who began to think that the study of art was a less easy matter than he had supposed. When they had looked at the "Immaculate Conception" long enough, they wandered rather aimlessly round the room; presently they found themselves in the long gallery.

Standing motionless before " L'homme au Gant " of Titian was a young man, apparently lost in deep study. Lil uttered a little exclamation of delight. John Bruce, for it was he, turned quickly round, and in an instant his face grew very bright.

" Miss Temple! " and he pressed her hand warmly.

She was very glad to see him, it seemed as though she were no longer alone in this great, strange city; she felt, too, that he had changed, that he was no longer the rather awkward young man she had known; he was more sure of himself, he had had some success, and was beginning to take a certain position in the world. He turned towards Mr. Smith, and for an

instant his tell-tale face was clouded.
What was this man to Lil?

"Mr. Smith kindly asked me to do a
little sight-seeing with him. Mrs. Cox—
you know, Mr. Bruce, I am her companion
—has no time of course to show me Paris.
Mr. Smith, this is the young artist of whom
I spoke to you last evening."

"Ah, indeed! glad to make your acquaintance, sir," and he shook hands in
hearty American style. "We are going to
study art, Miss Temple and I; would you
just give us a lift?"

"Certainly, with great pleasure," answered John, his eyes gleaming with
suppressed amusement; "I am about to
finish an important portrait, and whenever
that happens I come here to study Titian
or Velasquez; I cannot tell you how many
times I have stood before this picture,"

and he turned towards it with an artist's reverent admiration.

"Indeed?" said Mr. Smith with genuine surprise, for it seemed to him very black and uninteresting. "But, now, suppose you show us the real pictures, those one ought to admire; this one is very well in its way, I dare say, but, after all, one does not care, you know, to look at the portraits of people one does not know."

John Bruce was one of nature's gentlemen; he remained as courteous and quiet as ever, though the twinkle in his eyes did not escape Lil; she blushed slightly and wished, she on her side could appreciate the things he so admired. She followed his clear, simple explanations eagerly, tried to see with his eyes, and wondered that pictures she had passed by indifferently half-an-hour before, should suddenly appear to her so beautiful. John was in his element; he loved art passionately, and he had studied it with humility. Lil thought, as she looked at him and listened, that she had never known him before.

"I suppose it is because you were born an artist that you understand all artistic things—it is a gift of nature."

"Not entirely," and John laughed. "Do you know when I first stood where we are standing now, just four years ago, I said to myself, 'Are these the things they talk about and write about so much? I am sure I could do as well, if I tried;' so I did try, and the more I tried, the more convinced I became that I knew nothing at all, and that the old masters were really masters. I know very few people who, when they first see a Raphael, do not experience a feeling of disappointment."

" I am glad," sighed Lil, who was indeed glad to have companions in the humiliation she felt.

Mr. Smith, on his side, felt no humiliation whatever. "I tell you what it is," he said, standing before the Joconde, his hat pushed back and his hands in his pockets. "I tell you what it is, people have got up a sort of tradition about these 'old masters,' as you call them, and traditions are devilish hard things to root up. The fact is, between ourselves, they are dreadfully over-rated; half the people who come here to stare and to gape, think as I do, only they have not the courage to say it! What do I care for all these dingy old canvases? Look at this one now! who ever saw a landscape of that blue-green colour? I never did, for one, nor you either. Only this disagreeable-looking young person,

with her queer mouth and bad-looking eyes,
is by—what do you call him?"

"Leonardo da Vinci," answered John,
infinitely amused.

Lil on her side was blushing. Mr. Smith
was talking so loud, that several people
had already stopped to listen and stare.

"And he is an old master, therefore you
admire him. I do not; I mean to go in
for the moderns; I saw some pictures
the other day at an American's, worth a
lot of money. I mean to have some like
them, they are so bright—so bright that
the painter seems to make his colours out
of sunshine; somehow, turn one of his
pictures upside down, or sideways—it is
always pretty to look at — I forget the
painter's name."

"Fortuny?" suggested John.

"That's the man; it seems his things

go up in price every month. I mean to encourage the colourists, to have a picture-gallery that will make people's eyes ache! You must know the great artists here; will you take Miss Temple and myself to their studios? They none of them will refuse to receive a buyer with plenty of money in his pocket-book! We will commence by you, if you please; Miss Lil here tells me that you are a real genius."

"You are too good," answered John, with a sort of haughtiness Lil had never seen before in him; "but as I am only a portrait-painter, you would find nothing to attract you in my studio."

"But you will not refuse to receive me there as a friend—not as a customer," said Mr. Smith, who was quick enough and kind-hearted too; "especially if Miss Temple accompanies me."

"I should like to go," said Lil frankly.

"My place is in great disorder; I am going to move next week; but if you will excuse dust and confusion, I should be very happy indeed to receive you."

It was soon arranged that they should drive there at once.

Lil had never been in an artist's studio before, and she was infinitely amused with all she saw. John had by no means exaggerated, when he said that his place was in disorder; the lay-figure, half-draped, held out an arm imploringly, while its head was placed wrong side forward. Plaster casts were lying on the chairs, waiting to be packed; bits of drapery faded and full of holes, were hanging in studied folds; piles of studies, sketches, and blank canvases stood against the walls, while on the easel was displayed a portrait nearly finished.

It was a man's portrait, very simple in arrangement, with none of the tricks for attracting attention which portrait-painters so often resort to.

John Bruce's work was like himself, eminently honest; there was special sincerity in the treatment of the head; the man's nature was stamped on his features, and in his speaking eyes. That was John's great quality, he knew how to portray the character of his sitters, to give life and individuality to his portraits. Besides, the painting was solid and the colour very true to nature.

Lil stood some time before the picture, and then said, looking up,—

"I am entirely ignorant about art-matters, but I feel that it is a good portrait, John." She called him by his name almost unconsciously; it had become a habit with

Martha, who had known him as a boy, to speak of him as " John."

" I am so glad ;" and his face showed that indeed he was glad.

Then, while Mr. Smith, who was blessed with an inquiring mind, asked question after question about the technical part of painting, about the colours, about the price of materials, etc., Lil flitted about like a curious child: she peeped into portfolios, looked gravely at an " écorché," and even indiscreetly turned round the pictures that stood against the wall. John, after a while, noticed that she had grown quiet : he left Mr. Smith examining the contents of his colour-box, and went up to where she stood quite motionless, looking at a sketch-book. Her face had grown very grave and troubled.

" What is it ? " he asked.

The sketch-book was open on her lap, on one leaf was pasted the drawing he had made of her one evening at Mrs. Richards'; on the other was a sketch of some flowers in a basket; it was a hasty water-colour drawing, with the tints of the flowers just indicated, but she recognized it at once. The flowers she had received during those black days of despair, those flowers that had brought courage and hope with their sweet perfume, had been sent—not by Leigh Ward—John was the giver; she knew it now.

" Are you displeased ? " asked John.

Lil did not answer, but quietly replaced the sketch-book. The young man watched her eagerly; he did not understand the change which had come over her.

" How shall I see you again ? " he asked, feeling that he could not let her go quite out of his life.

"I do not know—I am not my own mistress; and we are soon to leave Paris for Italy;" then as she returned to Mr. Smith's side, she told him that they must go—that it was late, and that Mrs. Cox would be expecting her. Mrs. Cox did not scold; on the contrary, she was most good tempered and amiable; she kept Mr. Smith to dinner, and displayed her most dazzling smiles for his benefit. Lil, on the contrary was very silent.

CHAPTER V.

PERPLEXITIES.

YES, thought Mrs. Cox, as she mused over her plan, for which she had grown really eager—decidedly it would be pleasant—it would be a triumph, to present Mrs. Barnard Smith to that fashionable world which now so ignored Lil Temple. To show her, as her work, to hear praises of her beauty, which was of a quiet kind, never destined to cast a shadow on her own; to order the bride's toilettes, she, whose taste was acknowledged to be perfect. She did not conceal from herself that success was not absolutely certain. There undoubtedly had been some sentimental passages between Lil and Mr. Ward; but since the dinner-party, the young girl had appeared so coldly indifferent to him that it was reassuring. On the other hand, it is true, she avoided anything which might be construed into encouragement to Mr. Smith, whose visits become more and more frequent, more and more significant; but then Mr. Smith was an original person, and Lil's reserve seemed not to displease him.

During this time, the young companion became a far more important person than she had heretofore been. Without being herself quite aware of the change, Mrs. Cox treated the future Mrs. Smith with more consideration than she had treated the little nobody whom she had patronized; she still exacted services, made use of her as before, but there was a shade of difference in her way of doing this, which Lil perfectly felt and understood. She took her with her to the houses of her aristocratic friends more than she had done before, and without bringing her into much notice, managed so well, that the young girl had partners for most of the dances, and a place at the supper-tables. In spite of her better sense, Lil found this sort of life becoming extremely fascinating ; Mrs. Cox had calculated upon this, she meant to dazzle her, to make her feel to the utmost the worth of wealth and position.

One day Mrs. Cox said abruptly, look-ing up from a paper she was lazily looking over,—

" Why ! here is a long article consecrated to a friend of ours, ' Portrait of the United States' Minister, by Mr. John Bruce ;' he is on the road to fame, it seems ! Did you know he was in Paris ?"

" Yes."

" Have you seen him ?"

" Mr. Smith and I met him at the Louvre, and then he took us to his painting-room, where we saw this same portrait."

"Indeed ! you said nothing about it at the time," exclaimed Mrs. Cox rather sharply.

" Did I not?" and she went on adding up the week's expenses, which interesting work fell to her share. Presently the pen remained idle, and she became lost in a far-away reverie.

" What on earth are you thinking about?" asked her mistress impatiently : she did not like that far-away look; it belonged to that sentimental part of Lil's character, which it was most necessary to eradicate.

"I was thinking," answered Lil slowly, folding her hands on her lap. "I was thinking what a pretty story it would have made."

"What story?"

"If John and I had been in love with each other—long ago, when he was a poor boy selling newspapers to support his family, and passing his nights in drawing; in love with me, a rich girl whom he scarcely dared to approach, faithful to me in my troubles too, as a true-hearted lover would have been. . . You can imagine our parting, can you not? when he left me to come here and study, to work hard so as to become a great painter, to win a position which he might offer to his bride. Then our meeting here—not openly meeting, because of your prejudices against men whose gloves are not perfect, and whose

names arc̄ yet unknown. The tender love-
passages at those chance meetings of ours,
—vows exchanged."

" But you are mad, Lil !" Mrs. Cox was
seriously alarmed.

" No ; not mad enough to think that real
life ever arranges itself like the chapters
in a romance. Do not fear. I am not in
love with John ; we have not exchanged
vows—nothing of what might have happened, has happened."

" And he—is he ?"

" In love with me ? why should he be ?
If I were a man, I would not fall in love
with Lil Temple—a girl with so little
strength of purpose ; so easily moved here
and there ; dazzled with false tinsel—a
girl who does not know herself! I hope
he may love a different sort of woman, one
who will appreciate his fine nature, who

will be proud to be his, rejoice in his success, console him in failure, be always his support, and the happiness of his life. It must be a noble woman who is worthy to be a true artist's wife—one who would not fear hardships, privations and poverty; one who would not long for worldly pleasures, for dancing, for fine dresses, and fine compliments."

Then suddenly, without warning, Lil began to cry, and hurried from the room.

"Nervous," muttered Mrs. Cox, shrugging her shoulders.

When Lil said that she did not know herself, she said but what was literally true. What did she want? whither was she drifting? was it love or hatred that she felt for Leigh Ward? was she entirely indifferent to the sincere affection she had seen in John Bruce's earnest eyes? To

these questions she could find no answers;
they kept forming and reforming in her
mind, until she grew feverish and unhappy;
she began to feel a dangerous contempt
for herself, and a conviction that she was
too weak to guide herself; seeing no issue
from her perplexities, she abandoned herself to circumstances; what mattered, after
all, what became of her? she scarcely saw
where wrong began. Sometimes she fancied
herself the wife of Mr. Barnard Smith;
rich, petted, envied; Leigh Ward at her
feet; she would make him mad with love
—then spurn him, it would be her revenge.
She would turn from these thoughts hastily,
knowing them to be wicked, but her best
efforts could not make her indifferent to
Leigh.   She had pride enough, however,
to hide her passion; no one among the
people who frequented Mrs. Cox's, guessed

her secret. Mrs. Cox herself, though she was not quite easy on the subject, saw no cause for immediate alarm; nothing could have been more satisfactory than the quiet tone of polite indifference with which she addressed her lover.

For he was her lover; each day, the novelty of the situation attracted him more and more; he had very nearly been in love with Miss Temple a year ago; her prettiness, her natural simplicity had charmed his delicate tastes; now it was very different, there was a sort of mystery in their rare chance encounters. There was an irresistible seduction in the contrast between her cold manner, and the fire that at times flashed from her eyes. Since the dinner-party, when his neglect had so hurt her, since, especially, she had discovered that the flowers which she had fondly thought came from him had in reality been sent by another, there was deep concentrated anger in her—anger which pierced through her best-acted indifference.

Lil was not easy to approach during this time. In the presence of Mrs. Cox it was impossible even to speak to her. Sometimes, not often however, they met at some evening reception. On one of these occasions he went up to her, and said,—

"Can you not give me the next waltz? I want to speak to you—I must speak to you!"

"I am engaged," Lil answered coldly, glad to be able so to answer.

"Then the next?"

"I believe we are going away early; Mrs. Cox does not like dancing-parties;" then she added, looking him straight in the eyes, her own full of cold irony. "Take care, Mr. Ward, you are being watched, remember we are not alone; this is not one of the occasions on which you can lavish your attentions on me with impunity. Miss Blair is looking at you—go!—or you will be compromised."

At that moment her partner came to claim her, and she turned from the young man with a slight salute, in which she put as much insolence as a well-bred woman can put in such an act.

Leigh looked after her, until she was lost in the whirling crowd; and the look was not a good one.

CHAPTER VI.

THE POMPS AND VANITIES OF THIS WORLD.

QUITE unconsciously to herself, Lil thus became an object of considerable interest to Mrs. Cox's acquaintances. She who, at first, had been so completely unnoticed, was now honoured by looks full of curiosity, and even now and then by a few words of politeness. Mr. Smith's constant visits were rightly interpreted.

"I can assure you that he does not come for me," Mrs. Cox would say laughingly; but when she was pressed with questions, she avoided giving direct answers.

The boldest of these lovers of gossip attacked the rich man himself.

"Do you know what people say, Mr. Smith?"

"What?"

"Why, that you are going to choose a wife!"

"Indeed! and who is the happy woman? Miss Blair? I took her in to dinner twice last week,—she is very handsome."

"Yes; but so is Miss Temple, Mrs. Cox's companion."

"The prettiest girl in Paris, according to my taste—should not we make a handsome couple?"

The inquisitive lady would then say to her female friends, "I cannot get him to confess, but at any rate he does not deny the report."

Mr. Barnard Smith's fortune was so

immense, that notwithstanding his abrupt manners, his fifty odd years, and his slovenly way of dressing, he had been most eagerly run after by maids and widows of every age and description. That he should, after all, choose a nobody, one who was not " of them," was considered a defection. There were plenty who declared that there was no foundation at all for the gossip : Mr. Smith went to Mrs. Cox's because he did not know what to do with himself, he was lost without his accustomed occupations, and was glad to take the first opportunity of disposing of his time; these people asserted that sometimes he did not speak to Miss Temple at all in a whole evening. That he did not pay Lil any very marked attentions was true; he seemed quite satisfied with passing evening after evening near her, looking at her from a distance, or exchanging a few brief sentences with her. He had attempted to repeat the art excursions, but this Lil had refused to do; she had looked up at him with her frank eyes, and had simply said, " Do not ask me —I cannot," and he had not insisted.

Once, however, he had said to her,—

" Miss Temple, do you know that, as students of art, we are not doing our duty ? It seems that there is a fine private collection of paintings on exhibition previous to the sale, which all people who respect themselves ought to see. If I persuade Mrs. Cox that it is her bounden duty to go and admire these paintings in my company, will you accompany us ?"

" Certainly."

" Well, then I will see if your friend Mr. Bruce can be of the party."

" Oh, no ! he is moving, he would surely

not have time," Lil answered, rather quickly. She did not want to see John Bruce.

But Mr. Smith, imagining that she was still thinking of the torn glove, went resolutely up to Mrs. Cox, and exposed his wishes; she was most graciously disposed.

" And I want to present a young artist friend of mine, who will tell us what we must admire, and what we must not admire; a very clever fellow, a Mr. John Bruce."

" I know him already," said Mrs. Cox; " but—"

" But what? I assure you that he does not wear his hair floating on his shoulders, that he dresses like everybody else—better than I do—" he added, with a grim smile.

" Mr. Smith, I will be perfectly frank with you: if I do not care to have Mr.

Bruce come here, it is because I have a reason—a serious reason, for my conduct. I do not wish Lil to be thrown in his society."

"Why not?" asked Mr. Smith, becoming suddenly very serious. "Is there anything against his moral character?"

"By no means! I believe him to be strictly honourable, but he and Lil knew each other as children, I believe; there may even have been a little sentimental friendship between them—an innocent half-romance, which, if encouraged, might become far more serious, you understand? They are both poor, young, and romantic, and I prefer running the risk of seeming worldly and calculating, rather than see my Lil, of whom I am so fond—become the wife of a struggling painter. In time, when he has a solid reputation, should the occasion present itself of renewing the acquaintance,—why then—we should see."

Mr. Smith said no more; he began to think that Mrs. Cox, for whom he had never experienced much sympathy, was a sensible and kind-hearted woman.

During this time, the opening of the new Grand Opera was the theme of every conversation: it was to be the event of the season. Mrs. Cox, though she offered any price that might be extorted, could not secure a box for the opening night. She succeeded, however, in obtaining some entrance-tickets for one of the evenings before the beginning of the operatic season, when the house was to be opened to the admiration of a chosen few. In reality, Mrs. Cox cared very little for the Opera-house; for its paintings that had been so discussed, for its decorations which excited so much admiration and so much abuse, but fashion demanded that she should assume an interest, even if she felt nothing of the sort; and Mrs. Cox always obeyed fashion's decrees with cheerful submission.

Lil had been notified that she was to be of the party; she did not much care whether she went or not; she was in a state of apathy which comes to us after much painful thought, or over-excitement. This apathy did not leave her, even when she heard that Leigh Ward, as well as Mr. Smith, was to accompany them.

But when, in contrast to the darkness of the night outside, she found herself in the full flood of dazzling light, fairly in the midst of all the magnificence of the interior; when she looked up that marvellous staircase, with its grand double sweep of marble steps, its statues, its balustraded mock balconies, from which leaned beautiful women in gay dresses—the whole looking like some gorgeous picture by Paul Veronese, to which, by magic, life and movement had been given,—then suddenly Lil's apathy left her. There was something in her nature which yielded immediately to the fascination of what was beautiful, and rich, and gay with this world's pomp; she seemed suddenly to have awakened in some world of enchantment, which was her rightful world; she did not say much, but her eyes grew bright, and a flush of genuine delight rose to her cheeks. She had never imagined anything so magnificent as this triumph of French art, and that magnificence transported her.

She and her friends wandered here and there, to the boxes from which they saw the crowd,—for the "select few" had become an immense crowd, invading the stage—to the wonderful "foyer" where the beautiful paintings of Baudry, gems in their way, were almost lost by reason of the ceiling's height, of the dazzling lights, of the innumerable ornaments.

"What a true woman you are!" said Mr. Smith, who had given her his arm, and who was infinitely amused at her enthusiastic admiration of all she saw.

"How so?" asked Lil.

"Because you do so love glitter and show."

"If it is a crime to love what is beautiful, then indeed I am a great criminal."

"Poor child," he said half-meditatively, and with a tone of paternal affection ; "it does seem hard that, with all these fine tastes of yours, you should be condemned to poverty, and to earn your daily bread—

it is so hard for a woman to earn her daily bread!"

"Why should you speak of that?" she said quite pettishly. "Why not let me enjoy this one evening? why not let me believe for a little while that all this magnificence is displayed for my especial benefit? I may never have another opportunity of thus pleasantly deceiving myself."

"Why should you not have another —many other such evenings? It is an absurd fancy of mine, no doubt; but I sometimes think of you in the midst of splendour—legitimate splendour, all your own; with diamonds round your throat as fine as Mrs. Cox's—how do you think diamonds would suit you—and rich satins and velvets?"

"In the first place, Mr. Smith," answered Lil, trying to speak lightly,

" young girls never wear satins and velvets, nor do they put diamonds about their throats, even should they possess such."

" Young girls, no; but you will not always be a young girl."

" If we do not make haste we shall lose sight of Mrs. Cox in this crowd."

And she hurried forward. Once in the protecting shadow of her august patroness she relapsed into silence. Wild thoughts were dancing in her excited brain, thoughts in which mixed, oddly enough, scraps of talk which came to her from the passers-by ! severe criticisms of the beautiful building, mingling with extravagant praise of it by others. Then, presently, she heard more connected talk from two men who were following her footsteps.

" Acknowledge," said one voice, Lil did

not see the speaker, but she guessed him
to be a young man—"that there never
was such a marvellous display of magnificence and beauty!"

"The magnificence and beauty of a
courtesan; and to think that we have so
recently paid out over five milliards to the
Prussians! But we have forgotten that,
forgotten Sedan, forgotten everything but
our love of pleasure and our thirst for
novelty!"

Lil did not listen to the young man's
answer; it seemed to her somehow that
her case was that of poor France; that she
also had had her Sedan, that she had had
a heavy ransom to pay, and that the lesson
had done her no good. They were turning
away from the "foyer" when she caught
these last words uttered by the young
man.

"Yes—yes; but in all Europe there is not such another marvel as this! Why should we not glory in the good things that fall to us, rather than moan for ever over the past?"

"Why, indeed?" asked Lil to herself, and immediately she began talking rapidly to her companion, laughing and jesting lightly, until Mr. Smith vowed to himself that she was incomprehensible, but perfectly bewitching.

They all four rested in a stage-box which was by chance vacant, and the merry talk never ceased. Leigh Ward looked at the young girl's excited face, at her beautiful sparkling eyes, and felt that the opportunity that he had so long sought must be found that evening. It came at last; Lord Dolphus joined the party, and Mrs. Cox welcomed him with her best society smile.

"Fine, is it not? finer than our

theatres, I own—bad taste, of course; Frenchy ! . . . . Been in the ' foyer de la danse ?'" said his lordship, whose conversational powers were not brilliant.

"No ; it seems the crowd is dreadful."

"I should like to go in spite of the crowd," said Lil, " all that part behind the scenes is a region of delightful mystery to me, and I love mystery."

"I will take you, Miss Temple," said Leigh, "I have been all over the place several times, and consider myself an excellent guide."

Mrs. Cox looked up quickly, but she said nothing : Mr. Smith was absorbed in the examination of the velvet hangings of the box, making a mental calculation as to the probable cost of all the velvet used in the house. This operation was so interesting to him, that he only noticed what was

going on when Lil had fairly gone with
her cicerone. Mrs. Cox slightly shrugged
her shoulders; but, on the whole, she was
not sorry for the incident; a little jealousy
might not be amiss to spur on the more
than middle-aged lover.

CHAPTER VII.

THE OLD STORY.

Lil's flow of spirits suddenly gave way when she found herself alone with Leigh Ward, and she became very silent. Why had she consented to leave the rest of her party? she was acting in direct opposition to the line of conduct she had traced out for herself; still, she felt that she could not have acted otherwise. In the excitable state in which she found herself, prudence seemed mere insensibility; there was a wild throbbing in her veins, her eyes were dazzled, and could no longer see clearly.

"Well?" he questioned, looking down

upon her and smiling. They had left the denser crowd, and, instead of going directly there where he had proposed to guide her, they were slowly ascending and wandering at random.

"Why did you take me away? I ought not to have come," she said at last; but there was no severity in her voice, nor in her beautiful upturned eyes. They seemed to be wandering off in some enchanted palace; she did not notice the people about her,—they, and indeed the world itself, had disappeared from her mental vision, leaving but one man and one woman, Leigh and herself. She was, however, brought suddenly back to real life: she heard some one passing by say, "Two lovers!" She instinctively tried to take her hand from his arm, but he held it firmly.

" Why not ?" he asked in a whisper.

Why not, indeed ? Why should she for ever struggle against his love ? why should she fight against fate ? What had pride to say in the matter ? Who pretended that he did not seek her as his wife ? It was not true ! Still, in the hazy, half-unconsciousness which had taken possession of her, she had presence of mind enough left to understand that, since she had left Mrs. Cox for an avowed purpose, it was necessary to accomplish that purpose, to give at least a semblance of reason to her absence.

" This is not the way to the ' foyer de la danse,' " she said, half-smiling.

" No. Do you care to go, really ?"

" They will be watching for us from the box; we must follow the crowd, going up to the stage."

" There is another and less encumbered
way."

" But we must be seen," persisted Lil.

" That is prudent; there might otherwise be misconstruction and jealousy."

" Exactly!" said Lil, fully roused now;
" such a sarcasm sounds well coming from
you—you, who have shown such admirable
prudence throughout! O what a fine
manly virtue is prudence!" her eyes were
flashing with indignant fire.

" How beautiful you are in your anger!"

" Yes; that is a man's usual way of
escaping an explanation! Tell a woman
she is pretty, and you think her vanity will
impose silence to her pride. You are mistaken, and I ask again, as I asked just now,
why did you take me away?"

" Because I had a question to ask you."

They were now following the crowd

once more; it was not yet dense, and they could still speak without being overheard. Lil slackened her steps.

"What question?" she asked, under her breath.

"Do you mean to sell yourself to that man?"

She shrank almost as if she had received a blow. That coarse, harsh question she had already asked herself a hundred times that evening; to hear it uttered in a voice trembling with suppressed emotion, was terrible. But instantly she recovered herself, and said,—

"By what right do you ask me that question? you are not my brother; you are nothing to me!"

"By that right which—" then he interrupted himself. "Oh! I know that it is a fine thing to be very rich; few women resist such a temptation, but I fondly fancied that you were unlike most women."

"Why should I not, as you delicately style it, sell myself to the highest bidder? What has life done for me since I became poor? it is hard for a woman—for a young girl to earn her daily bread; it ought not to be so, but it is. I have tried it, and each day my poverty and dependence weigh on me more heavily. If some man, poor like myself—poor and brave—had said, 'Lil, be my wife; our struggle for each day's bread will be a hard one, but at least we will love each other, and bear our poverty together,' how I should have blessed such a man, how gladly should I have accepted privations; how devoted, how tender I could have been to such a husband; how proud I should have been of him—but no! such a fate was too

good for me," then, after a moment's pause,
she added passionately, "and it is you who
dare to judge me, you!"

They were now in the very midst of the
crowd, people about them were speaking
English; perforce Lil stopped, and the two
went on slowly. There was a sort of tem-
porary bridge of planks connecting the
stage with the pit; as Lil placed her foot
on this bridge, Leigh managed by a skilful
play of elbows to make an instant's clear-
ing about them.

"Lil, I love you—I love you! and—" he
checked himself suddenly; at that moment
Mrs. Cox's clear laugh reached them from
her stage-box; Lil did not look up; she felt
that her companion did so, and bowed
easily. How could he? Why did he stop,
why did he not finish his sentence as it
should have been finished, "and I want

you for my wife"?　But no, Leigh did not finish the sentence; she looked up at him. Her face was deathly white, there was not the faintest shadow of a blush on it—it seemed as though there were no place in this vexed and puzzling passion to call for maiden bashfulness.　Perhaps he understood the mute appeal of her white face; perhaps he did not.　His imagination was captured by this declaration in the midst of a crowd; by this mystery under the blaze of many thousand lights, in the midst of the noise of many thousand voices.　Long ago he had ceased to care for emotions that were not highly seasoned with strangeness.

The dreamlike haziness had come back to Lil; she could not think, she would not even try to reason with herself.　"I love you—I love you—" that came back to her incessantly like some intoxicating music softened by distance. More than ever she was in a dream-world, and the men and women about her were shadows. Yet, in a dim way she heard the various comments of the crowd; she understood vaguely that they were on the stage, she heard them say that it was the largest in the world; that its resources were inexhaustible; that the farther wall of the " foyer de la danse," was a large mirror reflecting the house;— all these words brought no distinct ideas to her mind, but she heard them nevertheless, and in an absurd way they remained on her memory.

Presently the crowd became more dense, still she felt that they were going up some steps; she even realized that the reason of the crush, which every moment was more dreadful, was occasioned because there was no other egress from the " foyer " so that the crowd coming down jostled the crowd going up; she felt that she had lost her footing, and was being borne along with the compact mass: women's frightened exclamations were heard every now and then; she did not scream, though she felt that she was growing very sick and cold; there was no air, she was suffocating!

"Une femme qui se trouve mal!" she heard some one say; she wondered whether she was that woman; she rather thought not, for she had not lost consciousness. But presently she felt that she was being lifted in a man's strong arms, and that there was great swaying in the crowd. She heard Leigh's voice whisper to her, "My darling,—my darling." She was satisfied, and closed her eyes wearily.

They were by an open window, the cold

night air blowing upon her, when Lil fully recovered her senses.

" Where am I?" she said faintly.

" Where you never were before, and where, in all probability, you never will be again," he said, smiling; " this is the first dancer's dressing-room."

Lil looked around; they were in a small room, mirrors were let into the wall and touched the floor; she saw in one of these mirrors that she was very pale; she saw also that Leigh was looking down at her, and that his arm supported her. The door of the little room was open, and occasionally people passed along the long narrow passage; but there was no crowd. Quietly she released herself, saying,—

" I can stand alone now."

" What pride!" muttered Leigh, as he watched her; she did not answer, but stood so that the air blew on her face; it did her good, it seemed to strengthen her, and she needed strengthening; gradually the memory of all that had passed came back to her.

" Madame is better—madame no longer feels incommoded ? " said a sympathetic Frenchman, bustling in with his wife ; they had been much interested in the young foreigner. Lil tried to smile, and Leigh with easy politeness assured them that " madame " was quite well now.

" Fortunately," said the wife, addressing Lil, " that monsieur your husband is strong and young—just fancy if I had fainted, my husband there"—pointing with a depreciatingly conjugal gesture at her diminutive, fluffy lord and master, " would never have been able to carry me out—but then, certainly I am heavier than you, madame,"— which was an undeniable fact.

Receiving no encouragement from either Leigh or his pale companion to gossip on farther, the good people, with a friendly nod, left the place, to discourse on the cold insensibility of " ces Anglais," and the overwhelming superiority of the French over all other nationalities.

" Confound them!" muttered Leigh, walking excitedly up and down. He glanced at Lil constantly, but argued no good from her white, set face. When that woman had spoken to her of " her husband," he had noticed an expression of painful rigidity about her sensitive mouth.

" There is no possibility of saying two words in peace here."

" Two words, perhaps," said Lil bitterly ; " but sophistries such as are common to you, take a long time."

" Lil, believe in me," he said with

great tenderness, taking her listless hand.

"I should so like to," she said simply, lifting her eyes pathetically to his; "I am but a simple girl, Leigh, and it is in my nature to be trustful; so much so indeed, that I am ill at ease in a part of suspicion. I used to think it such a natural thing when two young people—cared for each other to seek for the sequel of the love-tale in—" her voice trembled and she stopped.

"Listen, my darling,—I cannot here explain all that I must explain to you."

"What explanations are possible in such a case?" she said, growing once more excited.

"To-morrow you go to the embassy with Mrs. Cox, do you not?"

"Yes."

"I shall be there; you will give me your

card, and I will write names by each dance changing the writing, so that you can refuse all partners. I know the embassy well; there is a small conservatory opening from a boudoir; there I shall be able, I trust, to speak to you at some length. At the hotel it is impossible to see you."

Just then Mr. Smith's loud voice was heard; he was speaking to some friend.

"You are sure you saw them going this way?"

"Sure!" answered another voice, blessed with a Yankee twang.

Leigh uttered another impatient exclamation, then he said,—

"You promise?"

"Yes," answered Lil.

"Oh! there you are; what a fright I had! Johnson here said he saw you faint-

ing, but could not get near you—a regular
jam it seems."

"Yes; let me go to Mrs. Cox," and she
took his arm, she almost clung to it as for
protection; he was neither young nor handsome, nor had he an artist soul, but he was
an honourable man, of that Lil felt sure.
For an instant Leigh, with his hesitations and
his half-measures, appeared to her utterly
contemptible.   For an instant only—

"You are worn out, my poor child," said
Mr. Smith.

"Yes; do not speak to me just now,
please," she felt that at the first word of
kindness she must burst into hysterical
weeping; she bit her lip till it bled, and
allowed herself to be guided without even
asking where they were going.   Once she
looked back, but Leigh had not followed
them; she was glad of this.

CHAPTER VIII.

TWO LETTERS.

Next morning, two letters were brought to Lil; one was from her sister, a bulky epistle; the other was in a stiff business-like hand, she knew what the letter meant even before opening it; nothing astonished her much now, so it was with a calm of which she would not have thought herself capable some little time since, that she read :—

" MY DEAR MISS TEMPLE,—

" This is the first love-letter I ever wrote, and I dare say it will not be at all your idea of a love-letter. What I want to say is

simply this—will you be my wife? You
know I am not a man of fine words; I do
not even know how to make you understand that ever since I first saw you I was
attracted by you, and could think of nothing
else. It seems odd, does it not, at my age?
but it is so. I think I could make you a
very good sort of husband; at any rate, I
should try in all things to please you. I
once thought I would not ask you to be
my wife until I felt sure that you could
love me for myself; but I have a looking-
glass in front of me as I write—and I acknowledge that I do not look much like a
young lady's beau-ideal. All I ask of you
in return for my deep attachment is a little
affection. I know that if you consent to
marry me, you will be a good and loyal
wife; there is something in your eyes which
proclaims you incapable of deceit.

" I have been accused of stinginess. It is possible that, having in my youth known what it was to be very poor, I may have contracted habits of economy. In this case, however, there shall be no sparing. I promise to settle on you twenty thousand dollars a-year, and to leave you by will half my remaining fortune; the other half I intend to bestow on public charities. I shall count the hours till I can receive your answer. Perhaps it is ridiculous at my age to be so moved, but that I am moved and deeply, is quite true.

" J. BARNARD SMITH."

It had come. She held her fate in her hands. During the past sleepless night she had come to see pretty clearly into her younger lover's nature; to understand how entirely it was himself he worshipped, how incapable he was of sacrifice. She never thought of accusing him of deliberate wrong-doing. He let himself go according to the impulse of the moment; if the impulse were good, he was quite capable of follow-ing it to the end; if it were bad,—why so much the worse for those he found in his path! With this impetuosity, and strangely at variance with it, was a certain half-unconscious shrewdness, which prevented this impetuosity from ever interfering seriously with his private interests. It would have been almost better for Lil if she had fallen in the way of a systematic villain—one whom she could have recog-nized as such.

She sat looking at the open letter, trying hard to think, to decide which way her duty lay. But she could not; she seemed half stunned. If some one at that moment could have told her, " Do this," she would have obeyed passively, glad to be rid of all responsibility. But she was alone, and she must decide for herself. Then she remembered that she had received another letter that morning. She would read it before answering Mr. Smith ; it would be a respite So she tore open the envelope and read :- ·

" My dear Lil,—

" Do what I will, I cannot picture your Paris to myself. When I was a little girl I fancied that in Italy, when people asked for bread-and-butter, they did so in a cavatina with plenty of flourishes and trills. I have been told that this is not the case. On the same principle, Paris seems to me something like an immense drawing-room, where people are very polite to each other, where such vulgar things as hard work, poverty, or dirt are unknown, or at least kept out of sight. If you were to tell me that the houses are finished off with gold and silver ornaments, that the streets are of white marble, kept fresh and immaculate, I should be much less surprised than if I heard that vile carts rumble along the avenues, or that all the passers-by are not dressed in silks and satins.

"It would be no place for a work-a-day body like myself. I like a certain roughness; too much politeness stifles me. I like plain truths and hard work, just as I like cool breezy weather; but then I am a very prosaic person. And you, my Lil, are you not a little tired of your gilded cage? You speak a great deal about your surroundings and very little about yourself. I should like it to be just the reverse. If

you are not quite happy, dear, do not hesitate; come back at once. I am often very
lonely without you. I am going to set you
a good example: this letter is to be all
about myself and my adventure;—for I have
had an adventure, the romantic elements
of which were a rain-storm and an umbrella. But first let me tell you that at
this present moment, I have a light heart
and a purse lighter still. I have this very
morning paid off the last cent of the debt
that unfortunate school venture left behind it.

"I feel ten years younger in conse-
quence. It is true that the extent of my
fortune at this moment is represented by a
single dollar; but then, at my new board-
ing-house I have not to pay beforehand.
My penury therefore leaves me supremely
indifferent, since to-morrow—

"But I must begin at the beginning. This is how it all happened:—

"Just a week ago on leaving my work, I was caught in the rain—but such rain! The drops bounced up from the pavement and down again like miniature fountains, and I had no umbrella. Fortunately, I was passing by a wholesale warehouse, and ran in under the doorway, among boxes of boots and shoes. But I could not remain there all the evening; several horse-cars passed by, but they were so crammed that there was no room for poor me. At last, as the storm seemed settling into steadiness, I gathered up my skirts and my courage, meaning to run for it. At that moment I heard a grave voice say, 'Allow me, Miss Temple!' and a saving umbrella was held over my head. As I looked up I saw a bearded face, on which hovered an expression of solemn enjoyment.

" ' You do not know me,' continued the grave voice.

" I shook my head. Then suddenly, I let go my skirts regardless of consequences, held out my two hands, and exclaimed, ' Why, it is Dick ! '

" ' Yes,' he said, ' it is Dick ;' and the smile spread all over the face, and stayed in the eyes, long after all the rest was in repose.

" But you know nothing about Dick, or rather Mr. Richard Kirkland, as I now call him. It was so long ago; you were a mere baby, and I a little girl, when poor father took Dick as errand-boy. We were not as fine in those early days as we became later, and Dick used often to carry my school-books for me, or my skates ;

after that, he went to school himself, working his way there as, I believe, poor boys sometimes do. Later,—you were then at the convent,—he went back to the office as clerk. But at that time we lived on the Avenue, and wore fine clothes. Dick did not come often to the house, but somehow we met quite frequently, and the old friendship was renewed. One day father told me that he had gone to New York, and I heard no more about him. I do not think father told me everything, but I am not quite sure. I never spoke to you about this. After all, there was nothing to tell.

"The rain kept on pouring pitilessly. 'Had we not better walk on?' asked Dick sensibly; so I once more gathered up my wet skirts, and we walked on together.

'So you have come back to Lakeville?'

I said. It was an absurdly commonplace thing to say, but I could not tell him how glad I was to see him, could I? As to him, he was quite silent, just looking at me from time to time. He had never been a great talker.

"'Yes; I have come back as junior partner of the house of Small and Grove. And you?'

"'I, too, work for my living. I am in Mrs. Mitchel's millinery establishment.'

"'I think he held the umbrella a little less steadily; he did not speak immediately, but presently he said, quite low, 'That is hard.'

"'What led to it was hard, very hard; but the fact of having to earn one's daily bread is by no means the bugbear people would have one believe. It is invigorating, bracing, like a clear, cold winter. I think

myself less to be pitied than hundreds of
girls and women who cry and moan over
imaginary miseries, because they have
nothing else to do with their energies. I
am a great advocate for women's work.'

"'You are right, of course,' he said, 'I
can only look at such things from a mas-
culine point of view; it seems so sweet and
natural a thing to work for those who are
dependent on one, that we men instinctively
shrink from seeing women toil for the
necessaries of life; on the other hand, I
should not think dependence on a man she
loves, need ever be galling to the most
sensitive woman's pride.'

"'Certainly not,' I answered, with some
impatience. 'But men always reason
about such things as though all the women
in creation were married or destined to be
married. Even if that really were the case,

I do not see why a wife necessarily should not help her husband to make the pot boil, if she can. But the plain truth is that there are hundreds and thousands of women who are not married, and who never will be !'

" ' All of which means, You are but an impertinent fellow with your ill-placed sympathy.'

" ' If it is sympathy, Mr. Kirkland, I accept it heartily,' I replied, rather ashamed of my tirade.

" ' But nevertheless, Dick has given way to Mr. Kirkland.'

" ' That is but just ; our positions have changed. Besides, how should I know that Dick had not entirely been swallowed up in Mr. Kirkland ? How many years is it since you went away, leaving us entirely without news of you ?'

" 'You have doubtless forgotten how many; I have not. But let bygones be bygones; all I know is, that it is a great pleasure to find you again.'

" By this time we had reached the house.

" 'Good-bye! then you will not again lose sight of me completely?'

" 'No,' he said, and walked off quickly.

" The next morning a business-looking letter was waiting for me at Mrs. Mitchel's. It was nothing more or less than a proposition from the firm of Small and Grove to take the management of the millinery department which they meant to add to their establishment, which is to become the Stewart's of Lakeville. When I presented myself, the junior partner was as grave, as business-like as his elders. Every detail was discussed : my salary fixed at a hundred dollars a month. I am to enter on my new work to-morrow; I feel very important, but a little flurried too. I have not seen Dick—I mean Mr. Kirkland, since, but as all difficulties have been smoothed away from my path, I feel that he has not forgotten me."

Lil did not finish the letter just then, her colour came and went; it was as if fresh bracing air had been let in on her heated brow, which had dispelled her dulness of mind, just as the evening before, fresh air had dispelled her faintness. "What would Martha do in my place?" she asked herself, and the answer admitted of no doubt; she drew her writing-desk towards her, and quickly wrote a few lines, closed the envelope, directed it, then rang. A waiter appeared; she gave directions that the note should be taken at once, and by the same opportunity she sent word to

Mrs. Cox that she was not well, and begged to be excused from her usual duties. Then she leaned back in her chair and closed her eyes; she was worn out.

CHAPTER IX.

MRS. COX'S DISPLEASURE.

MRS. Cox was in the very highest spirits; she not only respected Lil's wish for seclusion, but sent her a dainty lunch, with an affectionate message to the purpose that she was to take good care of herself all day, so as to be able to go to the ball that evening. Mrs. Cox meant this ball to be the scene of her triumph. For she, who knew everything that went on around her, knew quite well that Lil had received a letter from Mr. Smith, and had answered it. As the hours went by, she rather wondered that he did not present himself; but then Lil, who was evidently nervous, had probably deferred the meeting—people of her temperament always were nervous under such circumstances. She spent this time in deciding on the material of the wedding-dress; she then made out a list of those to be invited to the breakfast after the ceremony. She was rather pleased to find that she could take such an active interest in the affairs of another; it proved to her that she was, in reality, a remarkably good-natured woman; she felt quite a delightful glow of philanthropy come over her.

When Lil received the message, and saw the delicate lunch, she smiled a little nervously; there would be a painful explanation; a storm of indignation which would be sure to last, at least several days, until some new pet scheme took possession of

Mrs. Cox's mind. The time dragged on painfully for the young girl: she was feverish and excited, the very quiet of her room irritated her. In the midst of her unrest, one thought was constant; she should see Leigh Ward in the evening, he would know what she had done, and—she did not finish the sentence, even to herself.

About the middle of the afternoon, a second letter was brought to her; it was short, she read it almost at a glance.

"Farewell! you are a good girl, and doubtless you act for the best. I leave Paris at once. Some day I may ask to be your friend once more—but not yet."

So, it was all over. She felt a great kindness towards the man who had always been so considerate to her; she was glad she had not done him the great wrong of marrying him. In looking over what had passed, she did not think she had been much to blame; she had never tried to attract the rich man whom other girls openly courted. His offer had been a great temptation to her, for she dearly loved the pomps and vanities of this world; in her moments of indignation against Leigh it had been a greater temptation than ever.

Mrs. Cox knew that Lil had received a second letter; this excited her curiosity. She allowed a short time to elapse, then she went to the young girl's room, and entered with a smile so beaming that it seemed to illumine the place; never had her voice sounded so caressing, never had a livelier interest been written on the whole face.

"Well, my dear, am I to congratulate you?"

Lil tried to answer, but somehow she

could not find the right words. The truth was that she was horribly frightened; so, in silence she handed the note just received.

The beaming smile faded instantly away. Mrs. Cox appeared scarcely able to understand the words, she read them a second time, and then exclaimed,—

" You have refused him ?"

" Yes," said poor Lil meekly.

" And why, pray ?"

" Because," answered Lil, roused by the hard contempt she saw in Mrs. Cox's eyes, "because I could not sell myself for money."

" Why did you not add, 'as you did'? More fool you, my dear! But there is another reason," she continued, getting more angry every moment; "you hope to find the reward of your heroism in another marriage—a fallacious hope, Miss Temple."

"My private thoughts are my own. I did not bargain to deliver them over to you with my time and my liberty."

Mrs. Cox did not answer at once, she was quickly recovering her usual composure, and said presently, with a little laugh,—

"To think that I should have allowed myself to get angry; that is a thing you ought to be proud of, it is the denial of all my theories. After all, I do not see why I should be surprised at all this; there is insanity in your family, that sort of insanity which leads to suicide—moral or otherwise."

Lil sprang to her feet with a stifled cry; the blow was cruelly well-directed.

"Pray, do not let us have a scene! you know how I dislike anything of the sort;" so saying, the lady turned to leave the

room. Before she had reached the door,
she had already asked herself how she
should get rid of this companion who chose
to have a will of her own, and to frustrate
plans in which she deigned to take an
active interest?

All that past, which friends were careful
never to allude to, which she herself, little
by little had grown to consider as something mysteriously vague—some dreadful
dream, rose before Lil vividly.

"Poor papa!" she moaned; she seemed
to see for the first time into that horrible
time of which none of them had ever known
anything; for there had been no letter,
not a word, which could have served to
make them understand what he had felt or
suffered. Finding himself worsted, he had
left the fight. Insanity . . . People had
pronounced that word before. But all that

had been so long ago, the past had seemed decently buried, that now to have it thrown at her unfeelingly—brutally, was horrible! All the troubles of the present were as nothing compared with the terrible sorrows of the past.

Then she thought of Martha, and re-read her letter. She so wanted to see her good, sensible face! Martha had always had that quality of good common-sense, that faculty of clearly seeing into things, of facing a situation, which had been so sadly wanting in herself. Lil had all her life seen a something, presented to her by her imagination—a something that looked like truth, but yet was not quite the truth. She would go back to her sister, and follow her example, put herself under her guidance. Full of these thoughts she sat down to write to her, but she only wrote a few words, then stopped—and Leigh? She pushed her paper from her, and held her head in her hands. She remained so a long time.

When she looked up at last, the early winter evening was already closing in. The dinner-hour came, but as she was not called, she remained in her room. No dainty meal was sent to her this time—she seemed entirely forgotten. After a while she slowly dressed, put on her one ball dress, which was beginning to look rather shabby, then went and sat by the salon fire to wait.

At last Mrs. Cox issued from her room, looking triumphantly handsome; there was not a shadow on her face. She had apparently forgotten that some hours before she had had some cause of annoyance. As she advanced she just glanced at Lil, who had risen, hesitating whether she should advance or not.

"It was useless to dress, Lil! I have too much sympathy for your bad headache to take you with me." Then, without a second glance, she went out.

She was not to go—she should not see Leigh Ward after all; she sat down once more by the fire, her hands crossed listlessly on her lap. This woman had vowed that she would prevent their meeting; she was powerless before this cold strong will, she might rebel, but she would always be subdued. What could her life be now with her mistress? the caprice—for Mrs. Cox really had experienced a caprice of kindness for Lil—had entirely disappeared and had given place to positive antipathy. How was this to end? It was easy to say "I will go back to Martha," but the journey was a long and expensive one, and Lil had no money. As she sat in the silence of that big fine room, she felt entirely dejected and forlorn; mixed with this forlornness there was a gnawing sense of disappointment. All through the emotions of that day, there had been, consciously or unconsciously, the thought "I shall see him this evening," and now! . .

The clock struck eleven, she rose wearily; it was of no use sitting there, watching the ashes of the burning wood fall away into white dust. She would take off this dress of hers, which now seemed such a mockery.

Just then there came a knock at the door: almost at the same moment it opened.

"Leigh!" she exclaimed, and before she fully realized what she was doing, she had sprung forward, holding out both her hands. She was so glad to see him! her weariness, her misery, her anxieties, all were forgotten—she was so very glad to see him!

CHAPTER X.

WAKING FROM A DREAM.

" So, it is all true ? " said the young man, kissing first one hand, then the other.

" Yes," she answered, looking up at him, and letting her happiness gleam in her eyes.

" You have refused him ? "

" Yes ! " she repeated simply.

" When I found that Mr. Smith had just left the city, and when I saw Mrs. Cox come into the ball-room alone, I understood of course. I slipped away as soon as I was sure of not being seen by her."

Lil did not speak; indeed she had

scarcely heard what he was saying; she saw him, she heard his voice; that was enough: he had sought her, therefore he had recognized that she was necessary to his life. He made her sit down, and then threw himself on a cushion at her feet.

"Lil," he whispered, "say, do you love me?"

"I do not know," answered the young girl dreamily, "whether it is love which I feel; it is rather like some strange madness, with alternations of something almost like hate, and something which, perhaps— I do not know—may be love."

"Which is love! why should you hesitate to acknowledge it? Believe me, life has nothing better to give, than a few moments like these—moments when all the world besides disappears; when two beings feel their hearts beat in unison, and forget all save that. Last evening, you did not stop to reason about your feelings, and you were right! we were happy—that is all. Our love made a sort of divine music about us, and the hum of the crowd served as a strange accompaniment to it; for we were in the midst of thousands, did you know it? we, who felt that we were alone in the world. There were not perhaps twelve people in that mass of human beings capable of feeling what we then felt. Love is the rarest of blessings; poems are full of it, and novels and plays; but the truth is, that in life it is rare, very rare. People who marry usually go through the grimaces of love, taking paste for diamonds, tinsel for gold; but afterwards they realize that the true meaning of life has escaped them. Love to be love, must be untrammelled—free; it must live as poetry and music live, and thus, it is eternally young and eternally beautiful."

"Yet," said Lil, smiling a little faintly, "shall we love each other less when what you call fetters are imposed on us—when —when we are married?"

"As to that, my dear girl—I for one do not mean to make a turnspit of Cupid. I cannot marry."

"You—cannot marry?" said Lil, turning very pale.

"I thought you knew that circumstances . . ."

"Then, why are you here?" she asked, trying in a helpless way to free herself from him.

"Why? because you attract me strangely; because my one thought was to see you, to be near you; because you are the sweetest, as well as the most natural of women! When I came in just now, I did not know what I should say to you; I only knew that without you all seemed a blank. Believe, that at first I tried to shake off this fascination, guessing that you shared the prejudices of the world in which you had grown up; but the attraction was too great to yield to such reasoning. If I am in fault, Lil, you must accuse the fatality which, after separating us, brought us together once more. Do not turn from me, my darling."

Lil shuddered, and by a sudden effort she rose. She held the back of a chair for support—she remained there motionless, unable to utter a word. But, as he was on the point of speaking again, she checked him with a gesture, and finally said in a broken, changed voice,—

"You see, mine is not a poet's nature.

I am but a simple girl, and I looked at life
simply; as those I loved and trusted looked
at it.   What you call prejudices are to
me sacred principles.   We therefore cannot
understand each other.   It has all been a
mistake—a very cruel one to me; but I
shall bear it, and get over it, I suppose.   I
ought to have known—I was warned;
only I could not believe that—" then
she stopped as though choked; a few
minutes after she continued passionately,
" Do you know that you have done a
wicked thing?   By what right did you
steal my love—a girl's first love—and
make of it a plaything?   But it was
deserved, perhaps, for I would not understand—nothing sufficed to open my eyes—
not your desertion of me when I so needed
affection—not the great worldly prudence
of your conduct since we met here—not

the hidden love-making which you would have been ashamed to acknowledge before the fashionable world! In very truth I do not know which is more criminal—my wilful blindness, or your disloyalty."

"You use harsh words," said Leigh, biting his lip.

"Words signify but little now between us; there is but one thing to do, you must leave Paris—or I shall. Of my own free will, I shall never again speak to you," and quickly, before he knew what she was doing, she had passed into her room, and closed the door; then she felt herself safe. The anger soon subsided, leaving behind a feeling of blank dulness, a humbled sense of deserved defeat. She did not cry; all the violence of her feelings had subsided; she stood by her chimney, leaning her chin on her clasped hands, and vacantly looking at her reflected image. That pale, dispirited, dull-eyed girl did not seem to be herself, but some weary listener who, somehow, could hear her secret thoughts. She concluded that there was some truth after all, in the satires of women-haters. Outward appearance —the cut of a coat, the fit of a boot, the symmetry of face, of figure, the charm of a smile, the sound of a voice—yes ! it was all this which fascinated women; not manliness, not intelligence, not heroism. Such was her case; she had never been entirely deceived as to the intrinsic value of Leigh's nature; she had known, even in her moments of most complete madness, that his was an aimless life, that his whole moral system revolved around a centre, which was himself, that even the artistic element of which he was so proud, had nothing genuine about it; he had the beginning of several talents, the appearance of art-worship; but he had never seriously worked at the improvement of his natural gifts. He was the poet and musician of drawing-rooms, with that sweetness, that surface polish, which is not incompatible with real mediocrity.

All these things and many more, Lil confided to the pale girl in the mirror. She questioned whether, after all, the feeling Leigh had excited in her deserved the name of love. There had been no tenderness in it ; it had come over her like a storm. It was not of such stuff that the happiness of a life is made. After all, was there such a thing as real love? Mrs. Cox asserted that there was not. Was life to all, a dull, blundering mistake, as it was to her ?

In the midst of her bitter reflections, she became aware that Leigh had not gone; that he was walking up and down, and stopping sometimes at her door. She wished he would go; the sound of his steps, though scarcely audible on the carpeted floor, irritated her; she was growing nervous; he ought to go. Mrs. Cox would think it singular if by chance she were to come back early, to find him in her drawing-room. Yet she would not open her door, even to bid him go.

"Lil! let me speak to you—for God's sake let me speak to you!"

She would not answer, but once more she grew troubled. In spite of all her reasoning, the sound of his voice moved her greatly.

Leigh had been entirely taken by surprise; he had felt so sure of his empire

over the young girl, that when she had
turned from him, he had lost his usual
presence of mind; his first sentiment had
been anger; then, as he recalled each word
of hers, the tones of her voice, the flashing
of her eyes—all there was of genuine passion in his nature was roused. Such love
as he could feel, needed the spur of opposition. Lil, gentle and yielding, would have
been a charming pastime; Lil, indignant
and defying, became an object of passionate
longings. For once, he thought more of
her than of himself; at that moment he
would have been capable of yielding even
to a generous impulse. When he found
that she did not answer, he grew half
frantic; and suddenly, without giving himself time for thought, he threw open the
door and entered the room.

"Oh!" said Lil, turning white with indignation, "I thought you were a gentleman, at least!"

"Lil," he said, in a voice trembling with emotion, not advancing, however, beyond the threshold; "I swear to you that until you give me permission to do so, I shall not venture to approach you; believe me, I honour and respect you."

"You have chosen a singular way of showing that respect," retorted Lil haughtily.

"I must speak to you; and this is my only chance of being heard. You shall hear me!—I am entirely dependent on my uncle; he is proud of me in a certain way, and makes me a handsome allowance. I shall probably be his heir; but should I displease him, he would send me adrift, penniless; my marriage with you would certainly displease him, especially as lately he has taken into his head to make me marry a ward of his."

"What is all that to me?" asked Lil; "our two lives henceforth are to be entirely distinct."

"That they shall not be! During the past hour, I have recognized that my love for you is stronger than my prudence—stronger than all beside; you must consent to a secret marriage. After the death of my uncle—"

"I will never consent to a secret marriage," said Lil resolutely. "If you were now to propose, not that, but a marriage such as is due to me, I should yet refuse. I do not esteem you; I even think that I do not love you any more."

"You do love me!" exclaimed the young man beside himself, and forgetting his promise, he went up to her.

"Go! you must go—think if you were seen here."

"I should not be sorry; you would be compromised, and then you would not refuse what I ask!"

"I did not think you could fall as low as that!" exclaimed Lil. Then she uttered a stifled cry; she had just heard the rustle of silk in the next room.

"Why, Thérèse," said Mrs. Cox in her clear, cold voice, "I thought you said Mr. Ward was here still?"

"He was," answered the maid, who was spitefully jealous of Lil; "and if madame will observe, his hat and gloves are still on the table. Perhaps—" and the sly tones ceased suddenly, doubtless leaving to a glance the care of ending the sentence.

"Impossible!" exclaimed Mrs. Cox.

There was a moment's pause; then

there came once more the rustling of silk.

"Leigh!" murmured Lil imploringly, forgetting all pride in her terror: she was pitiful to see. As for him, he stood leaning against the chimney, in silence; he had nothing to say to her, all the heat of his passion was gone in an instant.

Mrs. Cox lifted the drapery which masked the door, and stood there an instant, her lips parted, and a gleam of something not unlike triumph in her eyes; then, as neither of the others spoke, she laughed:—

"If you but knew what a singular tableau you form! O! pray, do not attempt to invent excuses. You came to pay a little visit of politeness to Miss Temple, fearing that she might be lonely; you talked of the weather—of the opera; do you think I doubt it? only—" and she glanced round the room, and then at the clock, "only you might have chosen the time and place better, that you must acknowledge."

Leigh left his place. He never even looked at Lil; as he passed by Mrs. Cox, he stopped an instant.

"It is not two minutes since I forced my way in here"—he would have said more, but Mrs. Cox interrupted him.

"Of course, of course! Pleasant dreams to you, Mr. Ward!" and she imperiously motioned him away. He bowed, and disappeared.

Mrs. Cox did not speak to Lil; she just glanced at her, not angrily, but with that sort of contempt which a good player feels for a beginner, who, having good cards in hand, yet manages to lose the game; then she left the room.

Lil knew dimly that everything was over for her, but she had no clear perception of the reality. She could not yet think it out; her whole mind was filled with one thought: she had loved Leigh Ward; how had that been possible? what infatuation had been hers? what spell had been cast over her?

She sat with this thought a long time, till the grey winter light began faintly to show in at the window: she then discovered that she was very cold and tired; she crept into bed and fell asleep almost instantly.

CHAPTER XI.

ALONE.

IT was very late when Lil woke. But the day was so dark and gloomy that, as she opened her eyes, she tried to persuade herself that it was not yet time to get up; she wanted to sleep again; she was afraid to think; there was on her mind the consciousness of something dreadful which had happened, or which was sure to happen, she did not well remember which. Who has not had at times that instinctive shrinking from full consciousness, that resolute turning towards the wall in search of blessed sleep and forgetfulness? Just then, however, the clock struck ten, she counted the strokes, then started up; Mrs. Cox would want her for her daily tasks—Mrs. Cox—then it all came back to her vividly, cruelly!

There was a look of desertion about her room; usually the chambermaid came in early to make the fire, and bring in a cup of chocolate. This morning the white ashes of yesterday's burnt wood were coldly scattered about the hearth.

Lil dressed quickly, then rang the bell. When she gave her orders, it seemed to her that the girl looked at her strangely.

In spite of herself Lil coloured; her story had doubtless made the delight of all the servants in the hotel, for Thérèse was not one to keep such a secret. To give herself an appearance of ease, she asked whether Mrs. Cox was dressed. The maid let her armful of kindling-wood fall, and stared open-mouthed.

" What is the matter ? " asked Lil, growing impatient.

" Mademoiselle does not know ? Why, Madame Cox left this morning nearly an hour ago ! Mademoiselle Thérèse was up pretty nearly all night, packing."

" Gone ? "

Lil grew very pale. Then the next moment came a feeling of relief; she was abandoned, left alone in a great city, that was true ; but there would be no scene, no painful explanations, no daily, hourly petty annoyances. Suddenly however, came the counter-thought — she had no money ! Something seemed to choke her—a sudden terror, such as she had never felt before; she managed to say, however, with some show of composure,—

"But there must be something left for me? some letter or message?"

The girl did not know; if mademoiselle liked, she would go and speak to M. le Propriétaire, or to the head-waiter. Lil merely nodded, she was incapable of farther effort.

M. le Propriétaire was a solemn personage, very correct in his dress, perfectly polite, and quite convinced that the man who could keep a large hotel and make it prosper, was possessed of sufficient ability to act as prime minister; his dignity accorded with his sense of importance. He came to Lil's room in person, and through his perfect politeness she felt that he brought his knowledge of the world—hotel world— to bear upon her case; and that that knowledge absolutely condemned her. He spoke in English with perfect fluency, and but slight accent.

"Mrs. Cox, on leaving—her departure was very sudden; necessarily so, she said—begged me to give you this letter in person, Miss Temple."

"Thanks," said Lil, wincing in spite of herself under the condemnation expressed in the tone of his voice, and in his very gestures.

"I beg to add that your room is paid for until this evening, your meals also. After that, perhaps you may prefer more inexpensive quarters; at any rate, I am bound to tell you that the rules of the house prevent me from receiving ladies unaccompanied."

"You need not fear," said Lil, flushing, "I shall leave before nightfall. Can you tell me when the 'Péreire' sails?"

"Next Saturday, at twelve o'clock."

She had, during the proprietor's last

speech, opened the letter and glanced at its contents. Though in his public capacity, the master of the establishment condemned Lil; yet, as a man, he was inclined to leniency. She was pretty, and that was a point in her favour; he would not, therefore,—having no clearly-defined notions of right and wrong, except always in his public capacity—be a hindrance in her way. So, having, as a public man, bowed and prepared to go, as a private individual, he turned and said in a confidential tone,—

" Should—hem !—any friends inquire for you ?"

" I will see nobody," exclaimed Lil hastily.

" Then it is to be understood that you left this morning with Mrs. Cox ?"

Lil was not quite sure whether she

ought to allow a falsehood to be said on her account, but the time was too short for any nice debating of the question; her one idea was to be hidden, and well hidden, so she uttered a faint little—

" Yes."

" I will give orders to that effect." He would on no account have shown it, on his well-trained face, but he was puzzled; he was undoubtedly puzzled.

When she was alone, Lil re-read Mrs. Cox's letter: it was short and to the purpose.

"I always said that hotel-life was convenient; I find it particularly so on this occasion. When you receive this I shall already have left Paris. I hasten my departure a little, and so avoid, what I particularly dislike,—a scene. I treat you better than many would under the circumstances. I shall write to engage your passage (second-class) on the " Péreire ;" besides, you will find enclosed in this note, a five-hundred franc bill; you were paid some little time ago, so you must be amply provided with money. Go back to your sister, and learn to make bonnets; a girl who has had such a chance as yours, and thrown it away, is not fit for anything better."

Lil sat for some time, her head in her hands, thinking out her position. Her ideas soon became clear, and her courage rose; she was not a coward, and this was no time for useless repining or sentimental sorrow. There is nothing like being forced to act, for dispelling imaginary suffering. Leigh Ward seemed entirely to have slipped from her life as she sat, pencil in hand, dotting down little rows of figures and adding them up. She took up her purse and counted its contents. She had, indeed, been paid not long since, but the money somehow had nearly all slipped through her fingers. Mrs. Cox had supplied the essential things of her wardrobe, but there were many small articles which she had not thought of purchasing for her; and which, when one goes to balls and parties, are absolutely necessary. Lil had bought these for herself, and being naturally inclined to extravagance, had chosen them of the most expensive kind. She had in this way spent far more than she had imagined, so that, turn her purse which way she would, two gold napoleons and some loose silver alone fell out. She would have to live a week before the starting of the vessel; travelling to Havre, and from New York to Lakeville, would be expensive,—how expensive she did not know, she could but guess approximatively; at any rate, it was evidently necessary to be economical. Having come to this wise conclusion, she set to work packing her small belongings, and preparing everything for her departure. She allowed herself to think of nothing beyond the immediate present; she would concentrate all her energy, all her intelligence to the getting out of the evil pass in which she found herself. Now and then it would dawn upon her, that her going back to Lakeville would be a sorry return home; she was a failure, this she knew, and it oppressed her with a sense of very bitter humiliation. More than once, a few tears fell on the articles she was folding, but she quickly dried her eyes and went to work with more determination than ever.

When the trunk was packed and locked,

came the question, " What now ? " Hotel-
life, even in a small, inferior hotel, was not
to be thought of; she must try to find a
furnished room somewhere,—anywhere out
of Leigh Ward's way. She put on her
bonnet and left the house.

It was one of those dreary, depressing
days, which those who live in Paris know
so well; days with which one pays for the
delight of sunshine, that bright, pene-
trating sunshine thrown back so merrily
from the white houses and glistening
pavement—sunshine which seems the rightful inheritance of the great pleasure-city.
In this dull winter half-light Paris shivered
and was ill at ease, seeming to have but
one care, that of anticipating the night,
which was to hide its unwonted dinginess
from itself. A black, greasy mud made
the crossings quite dangerous to the be-

draggled pedestrians; the trees in the public gardens and along the boulevards looked black and haggard, as though they despaired of ever seeing the sweet spring-time again.

It was not very cold, but the damp penetrated everywhere. Lil felt the depressing influence of the weather, and drew her cloak tightly about her; it appeared to her that hope had left the dull earth for ever. She felt strange and lost, not knowing which way to turn; she had been about the city very little on foot, and never out of the immediate neighbourhood, out of that "Rue de la Paix" and "Rue de Rivoli" part, where one hears almost more English than French. What she wanted was to get to some part where no English at all should be heard, save as a great exception. Fortunately, with her national American desire to learn, she had opened her eyes and asked questions during her long drives with Mrs. Cox; she knew that she must get across the boulevard on one side, or across the river on the other, before she could reach real Paris. She knew also—having by chance heard it—that when furnished rooms are to be let, a yellow placard hangs out at the front-door; while for unfurnished apartments the placard is white. With these two indications she resolutely began her search.

She went on and on, crossed the boulevard, frightened to death at the crowd of carriages through which she had to pick her way, looking everywhere for the desired yellow signs, and finding none. At the end of a street, framed by the two rows of houses, and having as background a picturesque hill covered also with houses, she saw a church, narrow-fronted, and surmounted by several statues. She remembered this church; it had been pointed out to her as " Notre Dame de Lorette." She would go towards it, and see if in some small street in its neighbourhood, the humble room she sought for might not be found. She felt strangely ill at ease during this disagreeable walk ; people stared at her as though she had no right to be there alone; her dress, simple though it was, was of a fashionable make, and she wore it with native elegance; then, the troubled look on her face, gave it a something touching and pathetic, which, added to its real beauty, arrested the attention of passers-by. Once, a man dressed as a gentleman, stopped and familiarly said something to her, which she did not hear.

With the unconsciousness of a girl accustomed to entire freedom and entire safety, she looked up at him with her innocent eyes full of wonder.

"What is it, monsieur?" she said, then quickly seeing his look of extreme amusement, she blushed crimson and hurried on.

"I thought Frenchmen were supposed to be polite," she thought to herself; wisely resolving that should this unpleasant incident be repeated, she would pretend not to hear at all.

All this time she was going on, and finding nothing; it seems as though whenever one is looking for a particular thing, however common it is supposed to be, it becomes suddenly rare. She was going up-hill now; it was a busy street, with shops on either side, many people hurrying by, and omnibuses with a supplementary horse helping to drag up the heavy vehicle. Before her, she saw a circular place, with fine dwelling-houses—which seemed to be there by mistake—and a fountain in the centre. There could be nothing for her there. She was on the point of retracing her steps to seek some less noisy street, when she noticed at her right hand a large iron gate wide open; this led into a deserted-looking street, where carriages did not seem to go much, and which apparently followed the circular curve of the place just beyond. She saw written up, "Passage Laferrière;" after hesitating an instant she went in. An old woman at the gate sat making little nosegays of violets in front of her flower-stand; she called out, "Fleurissez-vous, ma belle dame!" and looked at her with a curiosity that had, Lil thought, something good-natured and maternal in it. The place was delightfully quiet; uneven houses, some very tall, others comparatively low, all dingy, rose on one side, while on the other, mixed with ordinary dwelling-houses, were low buildings evidently dependencies of the fine buildings of the place beyond. It seemed respectable, Lil thought, and, at the same time, there was a look of universal shabbiness and neglect about the houses, which promised moderate prices; a shop or two, evidently suffering from the lowest possible depression in trade, added to the neglected look of the street. Several yellow placards caught her eye, but as they announced furnished apartments, not separate rooms, she went on. At last, when the curve of this singular street had quite hidden from view the bustle beyond

the iron gate, she stopped before one of the
tallest houses, and read "Chambres
meublées à louer." That was what she
wanted; she knew very little about Paris
ways, but she knew at least that at each
house there was a porter, and that it was
to that personage one had to apply. She
timidly ventured in, and knocked at a
door, the top of which was of glass; over
this door was written in black letters,
" Concierge."

CHAPTER XII.

MADAME BONASSIEU'S NEW LODGER.

"You have furnished rooms to let, madame?"

It was a stuffy, ill-smelling place, and very small. All the necessary articles of furniture were stowed away much as they might have been in a ship's cabin; the bed was in a recess of the wall, at a considerable height from the ground, so that, even while she asked her question, Lil wondered how on earth the portly " concierge " ever managed to get up to it, or, once up, to stow herself away on such a mere shelf!

She was indeed a voluminous dame, with a flaring red face, shrewd black eyes, and nondescript apparel. She scarcely heard Lil's modest, low-toned question, for at that moment she was saying, " There now ! the foot more pointed,—mind, if I have not good accounts of you next week, Céleste, why—!" then noticing Lil, she turned round with a stare and a sharp, " Plait-il ?"

Lil repeated her question, glancing as she did so at Céleste, a child with anything but a heavenly expression, who was practising standing on her tip-toes.

" You have no luck; I let the last not an hour ago ! I have nothing left but a room quite at the top of the house, not what you want at all;" and with a rapid glance, the woman took an inventory of Lil's dress, and calculated its probable cost.

"I do not know that it would not do," stammered Lil, speaking with far more than her usual amount of accent, as one always does when one is embarrassed; "I am in search of something very moderate in price."

"As for that, it is certainly moderate in price. It's my own affair, my furniture; —when my husband died, and I took to the lodge, I had more chattels than I needed, so I said to the proprietor, 'Give me some of the rooms up there on a lease; I will furnish them and let them on my own account.' 'Ma'me Bonassieu,' says the proprietor, 'so that you pay, I'd as soon let them to you as to another;' but he wanted a good price—proprietors are all so, they haven't any conscience."

"How much do you ask?" said Lil, who wished to check the eloquence of Madame Bonassieu.

"Thirty francs a-month—a franc a-day, and one over for the long months."

"Oh! but I should want it by the week."

"By the week! 'ça ne se fait pas, ma belle.' Attend to your toes, Céleste!"

"I am so sorry," faltered poor Lil, who was tired and disheartened. "If I were to give you a little more than the price, for a week?"

"Well, perhaps; paid in advance, you know."

With a little more parleying, Madame Bonassieu, vaunting her own tender heart, which forced her to go against her principles, at last consented, and led the way up interminable flights of stairs, talking all the time. At last, they arrived at a landing at the top of the house, and went along a passage with doors opening on either side.

"These," she said, pointing to the left-hand doors, "are mere servants' rooms, —half the size of mine, and giving on the court; whereas, in mine one can have a fine view of the street, by mounting a chair. Here"—she paused before a closed door, and spoke in a loud whisper—"is one of my lodgers. I know no more about him, than the first day he came. I have no faith in such shut-up people. But he pays regularly every first, and I fancy has very little to live on the rest of the time. He does not burn more than five francs' worth of wood all winter. Retired under-officer, or pensioned employé, I fancy. No visits, no friends, no letters—a mystery, in fact! But, bon Dieu! if one only took in people one knew something about"—and she glanced at Lil, who evidently puzzled her greatly—

" why we should never let our rooms at
all.   In the room beyond you, for instance,
I have Mam'selle Finette.   She calls it
her refuge for rainy weather.   Sometimes
for weeks and weeks we don't see her: is
it my business to inquire what becomes of
her during those intervals? Assuredly no !
She pays now and then; not often, it is
true.   I could turn her out, you will tell
me ; but then she has such a way with her,
such a laugh, and she cajoles me with her
' Voyons, Madame Bonassieu, voyons ! '   If
my Marie Louise had lived she would have
been just her age.   Then she is at the
Porte St. Martin ; and as my Céleste is destined to the dance, why, a recommendation
is not to be thrown away ; and she may be a
star yet.   You are not of the profession ?"

" What profession ? " asked Lil, somewhat absently ; for she had listened but

very imperfectly to the dame's rattling talk, being occupied in looking round the room, in which they at last had entered, and trying not to find it horrible.

"Why, the theatre of course!"

"Oh, no!" she answered, smiling in spite of her heavy heart.

The light came from a window cut in the slanting roof. There was no carpet on the floor, which was of red brick, except a little strip by the bed—a sorry-looking bed, shaded by limp cotton curtains of bright red and deep yellow stripes. There was a shaky-legged table, one sad-looking arm-chair, and two cane-bottomed stools. Beside these articles, Lil noticed a small stove, very rusty. On the wall, which was covered with a staring flowered paper, peeling away at the corners, were two prints, evidently the objects of Madame

Bonassieu's predilection, one representing the baptism of the King of Rome, the other a ghastly Napoleon on his death-bed. This last cheerful picture was placed so as to be seen by the occupant of the bed to the best advantage. Madame Bonassieu examined the young girl with a curiosity which every minute increased. How "une Anglaise," well-dressed, distinguished-looking, should contemplate taking this room of hers, was, of all the problems which her various lodgers had presented to her inquiring mind, the most perplexing.

Lil hastily concluded the bargain, and paid the week in advance.

"If Madame should want any little services," said the concierge, with the respect which the money paid inspired, " she may call on me without hesitation. I am a mother to my lodgers!"

Lil had but one desire—to get away from Madame Bonassieu's maternal solicitude. This she accomplished, after having baffled her curiosity on several points. At last she stood in the street, free. Having reached the Rue Notre Dame de Lorette, she hailed a cab. When she once more found herself in her room she involuntarily glanced about her with a pang of regret. Her eyes were still full of the hideous vulgarity of Madame Bonassieu's " chambre meublée," so that the pretty blue hangings, the gilt chimney ornaments, the flickering wood fire which shed a cheerfulness around, defying the dull dreariness of the day ; all these things assumed at that moment an exaggerated importance in her eyes. She so loved pretty things, she so hated what was mean and ugly ! On leaving the hotel she had ordered a cold lunch to be served, and there it was, daintily spread out on the table, with spotless linen and glittering glass. In spite of the serious subjects of sorrow, of which she had plenty, the thought that henceforth luxury, and even comfort, were forbidden things to her, was very painful. When her hunger was appeased, she said to herself that what remained of cold chicken and thin-cut tongue would serve her for dinner. She was irritated at these petty details, which had now so much real importance. She blushed as she hastily made a little parcel of the food, and put it away in her travelling bag. She was humiliated; poverty was even a more hideous thing than she had ever thought it to be.

Having looked about the room to see that she had left nothing behind her, she rang to have her trunk carried downstairs to the waiting carriage. But she was now a person of small importance. The servants, who had all been obsequious to Mrs. Cox, and even to her suite, paid but little attention to the discarded companion, who doubtless would give but an insignificant "pour boire," if indeed she gave anything. Twice, three times she rang, and at last, impatient of delay, she made up her mind to go in search of the help she needed. She ran down the broad stairs, meaning to apply at the porter's lodge. She had almost reached the last step, when suddenly she stopped, and clung to the banister for support. Leigh Ward stood a few yards from her, eagerly talking with the porter. Fortunately the short dark day was drawing to a close; the gas had not yet been lighted, so that she stood in shadow. She crept into deeper shadow yet, by a niche in the wall which held a statue, and there she waited. She had but one fear, that of being seen; but one hope, that of disappearing entirely from that man's world. As she stood there, listening, she scarcely heard anything but the violent beating of her heart. Suddenly an absurd thought struck her. If she did but advance a few steps, there where he could see her, if she were to consent to that secret marriage of which he had spoken, she need not carry away with her cold chicken for her dinner!

"But are you sure?" she heard him say, in a troubled voice. "It seems impossible! gone! and left no message for me, no scrap of paper, nothing?"

"Nothing, monsieur," said the solemn porter, who imitated his master's manner, and who evidently had his instructions;

"the lady would not even leave an address, in case letters or cards should be left for her or her suite. Everything is to be sent to her banker's. She means to travel for some little time, I believe, and to have her correspondence forwarded to her only when she arrives at her destination."

"I should like to see the proprietor," Leigh said, abruptly.

"Impossible, monsieur! M. le Propriétaire has gone out; besides, he could tell monsieur nothing more than I can, I was present when Madame Cox gave her last instructions."

Leigh walked impatiently up and down; once he turned toward the staircase as though he meant to run up to the apartment, and see for himself that no trace of the fugitives had been left behind. Lil grew cold with fear, but, as though on second thoughts he knew his determination to be useless, he once more addressed himself to the phlegmatic Cerberus.

"And you are sure that Mrs. Cox's party was complete; that Miss Temple, her companion, went with her?"

"Assuredly, monsieur," replied the man, with a quiet assurance in his falsehood, which made poor Lil feel very guilty;—was she not responsible for the lie?

"And they have gone to Italy?"

"I cannot affirm it for certain, but I believe that Italy was their destination. At any rate they left by the Gare de Lyons."

Leigh seemed to take a sudden determination, and hurried away.

It was quite over now, Lil felt that she should never see him again; that he had disappeared from her life, as completely as he disappeared from the hotel court-

yard. She stood some minutes, trying to
gather strength to leave her hiding-place,
but she was trembling so violently that
it was not easy to do so. Presently a
waiter passed, and she told him what she
wanted; he nodded, and called out to the
porter to send a man up for the trunk.
Lil remained where she was, till she saw
her luggage being carried down; then she
followed the man, got into the carriage,
and did not feel safe until the Rue de
Rivoli was left behind. She was dazed
and frightened; how she longed for the
weary time to pass; how she longed to
nestle close to Martha's side; there, at
least, she would be in safety.

Madame Bonassieu met Lil with a volley
of words, which, bewildered as she was,
Lil did not half understand; she gathered,
however, that candles and fire-wood had

been ordered for her, and that the " petite note " would be presented to her the following morning; likewise that the good-natured matron proposed to order a nice little dinner from a restaurant; which offer, when at last Lil understood it, was hastily declined.   At this, the esteem, which the sight of the trunk had excited, went down at once to below freezing point.   What! a young lady of her appearance meant to go to bed dinnerless! However, she followed her lodger upstairs, accompanied by the elf-child called Céleste, who was afflicted with a cold in her head and a habit of sniffling.   Her curiosity was more than ever excited.   What sort of person was this stranger? what was there in that trunk?   She offered her services to unpack it, and put things to rights.   This roused Lil to something like firmness, and at last she was freed from her troublesome landlady, who left the room highly incensed, and ill disposed toward the young girl.

To be alone and safe. That was such a comfort, that when she had fairly turned the key in the lock Lil looked about her, almost with satisfaction; the flaring red and yellow bed curtains, the hideous wall paper looked actually less vulgar than at first sight. There were draughts from the window, and from the ill-joining door, so that the one candle flared and burned down first on one side, then on the other; the red brick floor was cold, and the one arm-chair had a shrunken air of misery. But these were small matters after all, thought Lil, with an attempt at philosophy, which was not however very successful.

CHAPTER XIII.

DISAPPOINTMENT.

LIL tried hard to make the best of her forlorn position. But circumstances were against her. The following day was so stormy that, except to buy the absolute necessities of life, there could be no thought of going out; the rain came down in torrents, beating with such violence against the roof, that every moment the young girl thought it must force its way through.

Never before, perhaps, had the wretched room received so thorough a cleaning as Lil bestowed upon it; she went to work with a mighty energy, putting her mind to the dusting and shaking, as though that had been the great business of her life; doing her best to forget the past, trying hard not to think of the future. In a small closet she found an old broom, a few cracked plates and cups, a saucepan and gridiron, which probably had belonged to a former lodger, and which the landlady had considered too crazy either to use or sell. To Lil they were precious; she could cook her food on the tiny stove; all these petty details assumed so vital an importance in her precarious position, that they ceased to be mean or trivial in her eyes.

But once the work done, the room made to look as respectable as circumstances permitted; once the very frugal meal

cooked and eaten, the time came when
Lil was forced to sit down with her
thoughts. The rain still poured merci-
lessly; and every now and then gusts of
wind howled dismally around the chimney
stacks, just above her head. Then, notwithstanding her bravest efforts, she saw
all that had passed more vividly than she
had yet had time to do. The whole scene,
by which her one love affair had so
abruptly terminated, was present to her
as though she had seen it on the stage;
she heard Leigh's voice, then Mrs. Cox's;
the words repeated themselves over and
over again; she could no more rid herself
of their tyranny than, in fever, one can
help hearing some tormenting tune which
unceasingly repeats itself. And through
it all, the sullen, drenching rain, made its
dismal accompaniment to her thoughts.

To have nothing to do, to be quite alone—frightened too, at her absolute solitude—and to be incapable of freeing herself from these tyrannical thoughts !

Suddenly she thought of two or three books, which by chance she had stowed away in her trunk; they were English novels in the Tauchnitz edition; she eagerly pulled out one, and tried to read. But the story was one of watery interest, and she could not keep her attention on it. She heard her neighbour, the old man about whom Madame Bonassieu knew nothing, fumble about his room; usually he was so still that one might have doubted his presence. What could he think about during those long, dismal hours ? perhaps his brain had become benumbed, as a limb grows benumbed when the circulation is impeded. Then,

as she reflected about this poor being's
fate, it seemed to her a story as sad as
any she had ever heard or read; a man
who had outlived all his affections, all his
desires, hopes, or fears; who just existed—
nothing more, forgotten by the living: waiting patiently, uncomplainingly for death.
Perhaps he had had children, perhaps a
son who had dishonoured his name; such
things were not rare : if he had once been
at his ease, happy, surrounded, hopeful, all
that was in the past; he could apparently
just manage to keep soul and body together; he had not enough to allow him
a fire save on extremely cold days. What
could he be thinking about during these
dreary, rainy hours? There were no
poetic accessories to this misery, no " mise
en scene," as the French would say. She
had caught a glimpse of Monsieur Philippe,

as the concierge called him, and there was nothing attractive or grandly pathetic about him; he was an insignificant-looking old man, with a cowed, humble look, very shabbily dressed, and with a shuffling gait. But as Lil measured her own misfortunes with his helpless, abject, dumb hopelessness, she became ashamed of her own repinings, and she grew very pitiful about his fate. She almost wished that the next time they met in the passage he would speak to her, so that she might tell him that she was sorry for him. But she knew that he would not do this; his one object seemed to slip by unnoticed, to be forgotten by those immediately about him, as he had evidently been forgotten by those who had once been near to him.

Save for the moving about of M. Philippe, Lil heard no noise; the other

room, to her left, was still uninhabited,
and the other attics were principally used
at night. When, by chance, a step sounded
along the bare passage she would start
nervously, and look towards the door,
fearing that the lock was not secure.
What she most dreaded was an invasion
by her loquacious landlady and her imp-
like daughter; she dreaded the stare of
Céleste even more than the metallic clatter
of the mother's voice. She had never
before seen a child like this little girl, in
whom there seemed to be not only no
childishness, but even no youth; save for
her size, and her hair, which was plaited
down her back, it would have been difficult
to assign any age to her; she was sallow,
and thin, and knowing; she looked the
young stranger through and through,
seeming to have a precocious knowledge of

the world and all its wickedness, which put Lil's inexperience to the blush; she tried in vain to see in this creature the beginning of one of those dancers with their glittering gauzes, and eternal smile, which she had seen at the opera. These had perhaps been once like Céleste, practising continually standing on tiptoe, in the maternal lodge.

"You do not think my Céleste pretty?" had said Madame Bonassieu that morning, shrewdly interpreting Lil's shrinking. "But she will be pretty, and that before long; then she will be her mother's pride and support, won't you, my angel?" and as the angel nodded, sniffling as usual, the portress, seized with a sudden gush of maternal affection, caught up her daughter and hugged her violently; the child disengaged herself as soon as she could, and continued staring at Lil.

At last the long day came to a close; Lil to save wood and candle, crept early to her poor bed; a few hours later, she was awakened with a start; some one was trying her door, it was perhaps a servant mistaking one room for another, it was perhaps a facetious person who wanted to give a fright to 'l'Anglaise,' who, quite unconsciously to herself, had become an object of great curiosity to all the inhabitants of the attic rooms; at any rate, Lil was so terrified, that she remained trembling until the late wintry dawn restored something like courage to her; then only she fell into a troubled sleep.

Mrs. Cox had said in her letter that she would write and engage a passage in the "Péreire," and that steamer was to sail on the following Saturday; it was reasonable therefore to expect that on this Monday morning the order had already been received at the office; at any rate, Lil would go and see; she had no idea where that office might be, and Madame Bonassieu, when she questioned her on the subject, was quite as ignorant. The office of the Transatlantique boats! where did they go to, those boats? To America;—did the "Mees"—that was this worthy woman's sole English word, which she was proud to air—intend to go to America? not possible! that country whose natives she had seen represented in the "Tour du Monde," at the "Porte St. Martin"?—what a new source of wonder to the inquiring mind of Madame Bonassieu and of her bosom friends! But Lil was not to be daunted by so small a difficulty as that of not knowing which way to turn; so resolutely she went toward the more fashion-

able parts of the city. The torrents of
rain had washed the streets; the sky was
blue, and there was a delightful buoyancy
in the air: Paris was itself again. Lil too
was herself again; she smiled at her past
terrors; she would think of nothing but
pleasant things. How delightful it would
be to see Martha once more! it seemed
years since they had parted; in three
weeks perhaps she should be in Lakeville,
and all the past would be but as a troubled
dream. She made excellent resolutions as
to her future conduct; she would work
bravely, commence life anew, with cheerful
energy; she felt quite capable of it, she
would prove to others and to herself that
she was no heart-broken maiden, with a
sickly sentimental shrinking from practical,
real life. She no longer feared meeting
people she knew. Paris was such a large

place, that ever since their arrival she had
very rarely seen in the street a familiar
face. For instance, save that time at the
Louvre, she had never met John Bruce;
she wondered if he were still in town; she
did not even know on which side of the
river his new studio might be; he had told
her that he had chosen it because there
was an apartment joining it for his sister;
that was all she knew.

Meanwhile she did not forget her errand,
she gathered up all her courage, and
addressed a respectable-looking 'sergent de
ville,' who paternally put her in the way
she should go. The office was crowded
when she arrived, so that she had to wait
for her turn. At last she found a clerk to
attend to her, and she made her modest
little speech, which she had said over to

herself several times, so as to be sure of her French.

"Miss Temple—second class—retained by—what name did you say?" glibly replied the young man in English.

"Mrs. Cox," said Lil, feeling decidedly that her accent in French must be detestable. This saddened her.

The clerk turned over various leaves of a big book, then went to look in another big book, and finally returned, shaking his head.

"No such passage has been taken; but," he added consolingly, "there is time yet; we shall probably receive orders up to Thursday night, perhaps even up to Friday morning."

It seemed to Lil that the sun shone less brightly than it had done half an hour before. She knew that there was still plenty of time, but it would have been a great comfort could she have taken back with her the ticket; it would have been a foretaste of that getting home which each hour she longed for more eagerly.

Tuesday she returned; the same clerk gave her the same answer.

Wednesday, Thursday; she went morning and evening. The people got to know her; there was something in the anxiety of that pretty, pale face, which interested even the old grey cashier at his desk. Each time that she heard the negative answer, it seemed that some of her life ebbed from her. It was not however till the Thursday afternoon that she began to realize that Mrs. Cox had neglected to fulfil her promise; she would not even yet

quite give up hope; at the last moment
the expected order might come, she said
to herself that the cruelty of such neglect
would be too revolting; that Mrs. Cox
was in reality too good-natured to wish
her positive harm; it was true that her
philosophy was to forget as soon as possible all disagreeable things, to wash them
from her mind, as one washes off the
scribblings from a slate. Still a promise
was sacred, and she had promised this
thing.

The time during those days had been
wearisomely long to Lil. She had tried to
busy herself as much as possible; she, who
had always regarded stocking-darning and
kindred work as depressing to the human
mind, put her wardrobe in such perfect
order that it was a wonder to herself; but
when she dragged herself up to her cheer-

less room that Thursday afternoon, she was incapable of the slightest effort. What should she do, if the next morning, the place had not yet been taken? All night long that question repeated itself; even in her short, troubled sleeps, it was present with her; she would wake up with a start, frightened by distorted and fantastical variations on the same theme.

"Is there nothing yet?" she asked, Friday morning at eleven; the clerk had said that this would be the utmost limit for the reception of orders.

"Nothing."

Lil did not speak again immediately, she could not; yet it was exquisitely painful to feel that her misery was being noticed and commented upon by these people. Presently she said quite calmly, "Will you please tell me the price of a second-class passage ?"

" Five hundred francs."

" Thank you ! "

She walked out, scarcely conscious which way she turned. Before long she found herself in a square, the centre of which was arranged as a public garden. Merry children were playing about, and a few nurses gossiping together. She went in, and choosing an out-of-the-way bench, sat down.

CHAPTER XIV.

IN AN OMNIBUS.

SUDDENLY a thought flashed through Lil's mind, and at once her face brightened. There was, doubtless, a letter for her at the banker's; this had not occurred to her before. Mrs. Cox had evidently changed her mind about the "Péreire," and had engaged her passage in some other vessel. With nervous haste she rose and took the nearest way to the bank; she had often been there with Mrs. Cox. It was a place where she had made very complete studies of human nature under certain aspects—

studies in which Mrs. Cox had greatly helped her. "I always know the state of people's incomes," this lady would say, "by the smile Mr. Brown bestows on them; there is the pale and watery smile— means not worth mentioning; there is the respectful but reserved smile—it begins to count, but is still among the very modest fortunes. Then there is the hearty, good fellow smile, accompanied by a frank hand-shake—the banker feels that he has met a kindred purse. Finally, there is the smile such as he bestows on me, have you ever observed it, Lil? it transfigures his whole countenance. There are people to whom he has no time to attend, and whom he hands over to a clerk; when I go there he gossips with me by the hour, when I am so disposed; and as I like gossip—one always learns something new about one's species in a long gossip—I am often so disposed. I pay him for it; many a gold piece sticks to his fingers as the thousands pass through his hands. Bankers are like that cobbler's wife in the story, who measured the gold with a measure having a little wax at the end. It amuses me to see how very attentive he is even to you, my dear; I am sure that when I send my courier for money, he has to remember his dignity as American banker, not to shake hands with him!"

Lil knew that she was now one of those to whom Mr. Brown had no time to attend; she shrank nervously from this visit to the bank, but she had no choice in the matter; she had kept carefully away from all places where Americans mostly resort, for fear of meeting any of her former acquaintances.

It was not, therefore, without some trepidation that she went up the flight of stairs leading to the principal rooms of this temple of the golden calf. The green baize doors, with their double hinges, swung noiselessly after her, as though they also had an oily reverence for wealth, and dared make no noise. There was the same bustle as she had noticed many times before; the same clatter of high-pitched voices, the same rustling of silks, the same, or the counterparts, of the same pretty faces of girls and young women.

"I wish to know—" began Lil, addressing Mr. Brown, who was just entering his sanctum.

"I beg your pardon, I am so busy—could you apply to one of the clerks?" and he disappeared. Lil saw that his pressing business consisted in attending to an over-dressed lady, the successor probably of Mrs. Cox. She turned timidly towards one of the young gentlemen engaged in scribbling figures, and asked if there were any letters for her.

" Apply downstairs, if you please."

Lil was moving away, when close to her she noticed a very young girl, whom she had seen a few times; she was a bright, fresh, charming girl, and nodded to Lil with a pleasant smile; but her mother turned sharply round, and quickly drew the girl aside, saying, " Come away, Fannie ! "

Lil started, and blushed painfully; the meaning was unmistakable. Then as she passed Mr. Brown's private room, the wide doors of which were open, she noticed that the ladies with whom he was talking looked at her curiously, listening eagerly to the story he was telling them in a loud whisper.

She heard Mrs. Cox's name, and knew that it was her own story which was serving to amuse these good Christians.

She stood some time irresolute before the door of the lower office, but finally she went in, trying to be brave. There were no faces she knew here, and she went up to an unoccupied clerk and repeated her question. The young man took out a large packet of letters from the pigeon-hole marked T, and looked them over.

"Temple! Temple! no, there is no such name."

"Are you quite sure? would you be kind enough to look among Mrs. Cox's letters?"

The clerk good-naturedly did as he was asked, but shook his head; there was nothing.

"Should anything come for me—and I expect an important letter soon—could I

have it forwarded to my address?" asked
Lil, who shrank from the thought of return-
ing to the bank.

" Certainly—where?"

" Miss Temple, Passage Laferrière, 12."

" I beg your pardon?" he said, as though
he had misunderstood.

Lil repeated the address, volunteering
the information that it was close to the
Rue Notre Dame de Lorette.

" Oh! yes, I know," said the young man,
who was French in spite of his fluent
English, and who allowed just the faintest
smile to hover about his mouth. He wrote
down the name and address, however, and
promised to have any letters which might
come for her sent without delay.

" I wonder," said Lil to herself as she
turned away, "whether the place has a bad
name?" but she would not trouble herself

about such a trifle; she had subjects of far more serious anxiety on her mind. As she wearily retraced her steps, worn out, faint too for want of food, she kept repeating to herself, " What am I to do now ? " and she could find no answer.

At last, when she was a little rested, the answer came to her. A little silver alone remained to her, beside the five hundred franc bill; she had no object of any value which she might sell; to attempt to pay her own way home was therefore out of the question. As to applying for help to any of the American residents, that was not to be thought of, after her experience at the bank that morning. There remained but one thing to do : telegraph to Martha for help, and await that help as best she could. Her sister had no money, that was true; she had just paid off their debts and had nothing left, but Lil knew very well that what Martha would never dream of doing for herself, she would do for her; the money would be forthcoming, somehow or other.

Before starting for the telegraph office Lil wrote her message, which, after various attempts, ran thus:—" Send money for journey home. Am alone here. Can wait three weeks." She trusted nevertheless that Martha would be able to send the money at once. Three weeks spent in her wretched attic, alone, without occupation, was a prospect singularly distressing to contemplate. When at last the message was taken in and paid for, Lil drew a deep breath of satisfaction; she felt in direct communication with her sister. It was marvellous to think that, in a few hours, before she slept that night, Martha would

be reading the words she had just written.
She had paid for the telegram out of her
five hundred francs, and the change so
swelled out her porte-monnaie that she
could scarcely close it; it gave her the
illusion that she was a rich girl after
all.

On leaving the office she lost her way.
She was very tired, and the fact that she
had all her money with her—her life for
three weeks to come—alarmed her. It
seemed to her that the streets in which she
found herself wore a sinister look. She
did not dare to inquire her way of the per-
sons she met. At last she suddenly, at a
turning, caught a glimpse of the Place de
la Bourse. Her way was easy to find from
there. She felt greatly relieved, but she
had wandered so long that she was utterly
worn out. The busy air of the place, the

crowd of men gathered under the portico of the big building, the numberless vehicles of all sorts crossing each other with treacherously noiseless rapidity on the smooth asphalte, the bank messengers on their velocipedes, threading their way cleverly amidst the confusion of carriages and foot passengers; the calling out of the omnibus conductors; all this bewildered her, and added still more to her fatigue. She saw at a little distance from her a small edifice, with " C. G. des Omnibus " written up on the frontal, and a crowd of people patiently waiting about the door. Some omnibuses were stationed near by; others kept coming and going. Lil said to herself that it would be a great relief to go back in one of those. She shrank from mixing with the waiting crowd; she felt afraid of the official with a gilt band on his cap and

a metal whistle about his neck, who
seemed to treat all these people with a
sort of military contempt; but her fatigue
got the better of her timidity, and she
entered the bureau. Another official
was seated behind a counter, with quan-
tities of different-coloured tickets before
him.

"Could I find an omnibus to take me to
the Rue Notre Dame de Lorette?" inquired
Lil, feeling that every one was looking at
her.

"Place Pigalle—Halle aux Vins; it
passes by the Church;" and he pushed her
a bit of coloured paper with a number on
it. Lil knew nothing whatever about Paris
omnibuses and their regulations; but as
she picked up the bit of pasteboard, she
took out her purse and asked how much it
was. The man stared at her; then, seeing

that she was a stranger, and pitying her for that inferiority, deigned to explain that she was not to pay until she had taken her place; that she had better go outside, look out for a chocolate-coloured omnibus, and when her number was called out, jump in.

Lil, blushing deeply, hastened to take her place among the waiting crowd. A young woman, rather too flashily dressed, stood next to her, and examined her with persevering attention. She had been one of those who had seemed most amused at her ignorance of omnibuses and their ways. Presently she said good-naturedly—

"You know, you need not fidget yourself. I am going to take the same omnibus as you. All you will have to do will be to follow me; your number is next to mine."

"Oh, thank you!" exclaimed Lil, greatly relieved; for, in spite of her best efforts, she could not make out what the man of the whistle screamed out each time.

It was not long before the chocolate-coloured omnibus arrived, and Lil soon found herself seated by her over-dressed protectress.

"Your places!" shouted the conductor.

Lil was embarrassed; she did not know how much it was, and she shrank from asking the young woman by her side. So she drew out her purse, which she felt attracted universal attention on account of its plethoric appearance; she tried to find a small coin, but her fingers were stiff from nervousness; at last it was a gold piece which she pulled out. The conductor grumbled between his teeth at having to make so much change, but counted it out nevertheless. Lil caught the eye of a benevolent-looking old gentleman in the far-off corner, who gently shook his head in evident disapprobation of so well filled a purse in an omnibus. It is astonishing what interest people in public conveyances feel in each other! Lil hastily put back her purse, and when she received the change, she slipped it into an outside pocket of her dress, meaning to keep her hand over it; this she religiously did. She had a left-hand neighbour in a blouse, who smelt of garlic, and inspired her with no great confidence.

They had been rumbling along for some time, and Lil was recovering her composure, when, at a street turning, the omnibus caught the wheel of a small carriage, and tipped it over as neatly as though it had been done on purpose. Immediately there was a crowd, the coachman of the unlucky cab sprang to his feet, and, rubbing himself, indulged in a volley of oaths and imprecations. Meanwhile the two screaming women in the carriage were dragged out more terrified than hurt, and the confusion was made still more complete by the plunging and rearing of the frightened omnibus horses.

Lil was so placed that she had seen everything, and had been exceedingly alarmed. If she could but get out! she hated omnibuses, and vowed she would never venture in one again. She noticed that one of the passengers was preparing to leave, and she quickly followed him. She knew that she was not far from her destination; she no longer felt her fatigue, she was only too glad to get away from her garlic-loving neighbour. She wondered why all these people kept the windows so hermetically closed? She turned round after she was at some little distance, and saw that the omnibus had disengaged itself from the crowd, and was dashing along as though its ideal of life had been to upset as many cabs as it conveniently could.

It was not until she had quite recovered from her fright that Lil remembered her money; she felt quickly in her outside pocket, the change was all safe—garlic and honesty were not, after all, incompatible. Then she thought of her purse. She wore a long, tight over-dress which rendered pickpocketing a difficult operation; but as she was about to lift up this over-dress,

she felt something strange: it was a deep
slit in the stuff, just above the pocket.
She stopped suddenly, and hastily felt for
her precious porte-monnaie,—it was gone.

END OF VOL. II.

GILBERT AND RIVINGTON, PRINTERS, ST. JOHN'S SQUARE, LONDON.